**The Patient**

The Earl started to walk, at first quickly, then he ran.

Ansella was on the other side of the Tower.

She was looking over the balustrade down into the moat.

With the swiftness of an athlete, the Earl reached her and put his arms around her.

"What are you doing? Why did you come here?" he asked.

She put out her hands to push him away from her.

"You are . . . not to . . . stop me," she said. "I would . . . rather . . . die than . . . live without . . . you . . ."

## *A Camfield Novel of Love*
## *by Barbara Cartland*

---

Camfield Place,
Hatfield
Hertfordshire,
England

Dearest Reader,

Camfield Novels of Love mark a very exciting era
of my books with Jove. They have already published
nearly two hundred of my titles since they became my
first publisher in America, and now all my original
paperback romances in the future will be published
exclusively by them.

As you already know, Camfield Place in Hertfordshire is my home, which originally existed in 1275,
but was rebuilt in 1867 by the grandfather of Beatrix
Potter.

It was here in this lovely house, with the best view
in the county, that she wrote *The Tale of Peter Rabbit*.
Mr. McGregor's garden is exactly as she described it.
The door in the wall that the fat little rabbit could not
squeeze underneath and the goldfish pool where the
white cat sat twitching its tail are still there.

I had Camfield Place blessed when I came here in
1950 and was so happy with my husband until he
died, and now with my children and grandchildren,
that I know the atmosphere is filled with love and we
have all been very lucky.

It is easy here to write of love and I know you will
enjoy the Camfield Novels of Love. Their plots are
definitely exciting and the covers very romantic. They
come to you, like all my books, with love.

Bless you,

# CAMFIELD NOVELS OF LOVE
## by Barbara Cartland

A NEW CAMFIELD NOVEL OF LOVE BY

# Barbara Cartland

## The Patient Bridegroom

**J**

**JOVE BOOKS, NEW YORK**

THE PATIENT BRIDEGROOM

A Jove Book / published by arrangement with
the author

PRINTING HISTORY
Jove edition / May 1995

ISBN: 0-515-11615-7

A JOVE BOOK®
Jove Books are published by The Berkley Publishing Group,
200 Madison Avenue, New York, New York 10016.
JOVE and the "J" design are trademarks
belonging to Jove Publications, Inc.

PRINTED IN THE UNITED STATES OF AMERICA

10  9  8  7  6  5  4  3  2  1

# Author's Note

THE Earl of Mayo was the first Viceroy to be really loved by the Indian people.

He was not only extremely handsome, tall, and broad-shouldered, but he had an infectious enthusiasm, a gaiety, and with it a kindness of heart, which the Indians found irresistible.

Everything I have written about him in this story is true.

After his death he was always referred to as the "Ideal Viceroy."

I have known three Viceroys.

Lord Curzon, who was brilliant and intelligent, saved for India and for ourselves their beautiful Temples and buildings, which had been neglected for a long time and were gradually being lost to posterity.

The Marquis of Willingdon had not the qualifications and personality of his predecessor, but he was charming, everyone liked him, and he became popular with the people.

He very nearly was my Father-in-Law.

Earl Mountbatten of Burma was the last Viceroy and in many ways resembled the Earl of Mayo.

He was exceedingly handsome, well-built, and invariably impressive.

At the same time, he had the same charm, charisma, and enthusiasm for the people he ruled which made them adore him.

Although he went out to give India back to its people, they cried when he left them and paid him the amazing and extraordinary compliment of when he handed them over their own country, they asked him to stay on as their First Governor General.

As Pundit Nehru said in his speech at the Banquet on the last evening before Mountbatten left, "Wherever you have gone you have brought solace, hope, and encouragement. Is it surprising, therefore, that the people of India love you?"

# *chapter one*

# 1872

"I DO not believe it!"

"I am afraid, My Lord, that is the truth, unpleasant as it may be," the Solicitor replied.

The Earl of Rayburne could only stare at the man with an expression in his eyes which was even more dramatic than the way he had spoken.

"But surely," he said after an uncomfortable pause, "you could have written to me."

"We did not know things were as bad as they appear now," the Solicitor replied, "and in any case, Your Lordship had given Mr. Basil Burne Power of Attorney. Therefore whatever he did was entirely within the Law."

The Earl could not think of anything to say.

He had come back from India looking forward to living on his Estate.

He had supposed that everything would be exactly the same as when he left.

*1*

His Father had died in 1868, and he had come into the title, which was a very old one.

Rayburne Castle and its huge Estate in Oxfordshire was one of the beauty spots of the area.

When Michael Burne left Oxford he had joined the Household Brigade in which his family had served for generations.

He was, however, thrilled and delighted when later in the same year he was asked by his Cousin, the new Viceroy of India, to go out and join him.

It had been a great surprise when the Earl of Mayo had been appointed by Mr. Benjamin Disraeli after Lord Lawrence's retirement.

He was unknown to most of the English people.

But Mr. Disraeli was relying, as he had done so often before, on his intuition, and it proved to be a stroke of genius.

One thing everyone knew about the Earl of Mayo was that he was a brilliantly successful Master of the Kildare Hunt.

His young relative, Michael Burne, an outstanding horseman, was a frequent visitor to the Earl's house in Ireland.

In a way Michael closely resembled the Earl, who, tall and broad-shouldered, was a fine figure of a man.

He had both a strong determination and a great sense of humour.

His enthusiasm and his gaiety gave him a magnetism which made him friends wherever he went.

To the young Earl of Rayburne, to be in India with a man he greatly admired and whose friendship had coloured his boyhood was an invitation he could not resist.

When he looked round his broad acres which surrounded the Castle, everything seemed to be in order.

There appeared to be nothing which especially needed attention, and he could see no reason why he should not go to India.

Everything was made easier when his Father's brother, the Honorable Basil Burne, offered to look after the Castle and Estate in his absence.

"That is very kind of you, Uncle Basil," he said. "You are quite sure it will not be a nuisance rather than a pleasure?"

"I think I have been in London long enough," Basil Burne replied. "It will do me good to be in the country, and I can look after everything for you, so you need have no worries."

The Earl then gave him Power of Attorney and set off on a tedious voyage which took months, as it then meant going round the Cape.

He knew that at the end of it he would find an adventure such as he had never had the opportunity of enjoying before.

He arrived in India to find that his relative had already begun to win a popularity that no previous Viceroy had ever enjoyed.

Mayo's commanding presence, his smile, his joyous vigour and enthusiasm, appealed to the Indians.

They also appreciated the magnificence of his entertainments.

Lord Lawrence had been rather austere and very reluctant to spend any money.

The Earl and his wife brought back gaiety and glamour to Government House.

The fact that he had appointed a young and high-spirited staff made things very much easier than they had been before.

Michael was entranced from the very moment he arrived.

The new Viceroy had been considerably helped by the fact that the Government at home had changed while he was actually on his voyage to Calcutta.

He was a Conservative, of course, like Disraeli, but a

Liberal Government under Gladstone had just come into power.

This might have been an embarrassment.

Instead, it was a help, because the Liberals did not seem inclined to interfere in any way in Indian affairs.

This gave the Viceroy a free hand.

People had sneered and said he would have no idea how to handle such a large country.

It was, however, his experience in Ireland and his sympathy for the peasants of his own country which made him such an outstanding Viceroy.

He was particularly worried about famine.

This was something he had already encountered in the *"Hungry Forties"* in Ireland.

He also wished India to have schools and hospitals as well as railways, canals, and more roads.

He wanted also to see everything for himself, which was another reason why he had invited his young friend Michael to join him.

Much of his travelling about the country was done on horseback.

The only ADC who could keep up with him was Michael, and they often rode eighty miles a day.

Although he was not aware of it at the time, Michael Burne was learning to command people as well as his relative did.

The quality the Viceroy looked for was, as he put it himself: "An enthusiasm which makes a man believe in the possibility of improvement and strives to obtain it."

It was not long before Michael developed the same enthusiasm that his Chief possessed so abundantly.

He was soon entrusted with difficult assignments which the other ADC's were not keen on undertaking.

Everything seemed to be going well for the first four years of the Viceroy's reign.

He had two more years to serve, and it appeared as if he would be, without doubt, the most successful and the most loved Viceroy there had ever been.

It was then in February 1872 that the Viceroy arranged a visit to the Andaman Islands and a tour of the convict settlement in Port Blair.

It was the ADC's job to see that the most stringent security measures had been taken, and everything went off well.

In the afternoon the Viceroy visited another island of the group.

Then, when the official day's arrangements were over, he crossed to the principal island and climbed up Mount Harriet.

Only Michael was eager to go with him.

It was a stiff climb to an altitude of more than a thousand feet.

The two men refused ponies and reached the top.

They sat down for ten minutes to admire the sunset, the Viceroy exclaiming:

"How beautiful, how very beautiful!"

By the time the party descended back to the waterfront, it was dark.

The launch was waiting to take the Viceroy back to his ship.

The torch-bearers led the way and the Viceroy walked between Michael and the Chief Commissioner of the Andamans.

Just as the Viceroy was stepping forward to board the launch, the Commissioner gave an order.

The guards who had cordoned off the pier opened their ranks to let him through.

Before they could close up again, a tall Pathan rushed through the opening and jumped, as someone said: "like a tiger," on the Viceroy's back.

He stabbed him twice between the shoulders.

The man was dragged away but the Viceroy staggered to the side of the pier.

He raised himself out of the shallow water, saying:

"They have done it!"

A few minutes later he collapsed and the back of his coat was dark with blood.

He was lifted into the launch, but by the time the ship was reached he was dead.

To Michael it was a nightmare.

He could hardly believe what had happened.

The man he had loved and admired would never again say to him:

"Come on, Michael, you and I can do it together."

After the Funeral his one thought was to get away from his memories and what had been the happiest time of his life.

He returned home.

The voyage home was very different from his passage out to India.

The Suez Canal had been opened in 1869, the year following his arrival.

Now the new ships of the P. & O. took only a little over seventeen days to reach England.

Michael had everything he possessed packed and went aboard the first available ship.

His thoughts were still on the dead Viceroy.

He was in Michael's mind "the ideal Viceroy."

That, later, was what one of his most distinguished successors was to call him.

It did not, however, ease Michael's sense of loss.

He thought never again would he be with someone who could arouse in him an enthusiasm and a sense of gaiety in everything he undertook.

By the time the ship in which he was sailing had reached Tilbury, the first agony had softened a little.

He was now looking forward to seeing again his own Castle and Estate.

He felt sure that his Uncle would, as he had promised, have kept everything in perfect order.

He would go first to the Castle which had been his home since his birth, and find it exactly as he had left it.

The servants who had looked after him and called him "Master Michael" would be there.

He would ride the horses of which his Father had always had a full and outstanding Stable.

As Michael had left India so hurriedly, he had not arranged for anyone to meet him.

After the short journey from Tilbury to Central London, he took a train to Oxford and engaged a Post-Chaise to take him out to Rayburne Castle.

He paid for the best Chaise available, which was drawn by two horses.

He arrived at the Castle in under an hour.

He thought as he entered the drive that the lodges appeared to be empty, which surprised him.

The drive itself seemed rough and uncared for.

When he saw the Castle, it seemed for a moment, in the sunshine, to look as it had always done, outstandingly beautiful silhouetted against the trees behind it.

It had been a Castle since the Thirteenth Century, but each generation of Rayburnes had added to it and in their own way improved it.

Finally in the Eighteenth Century the Tenth Earl had the whole façade altered.

The original Castle stood at one end of it.

The rest of the building, which by now was now very symmetrical, was given a new façade.

It made it not only beautiful but far more impressive.

The renovation was designed by the Adam Brothers, who were known as the greatest architects of their time.

Now, with the sunshine glittering on the windows, the young Earl felt his pride swelling up within him.

Not even in India had he seen a Palace more impressive or in more exquisite taste than his own home.

The Post-Chaise carried him over the bridge which spanned the lake and into the Courtyard outside the front door.

The Earl got out to pay the man and give him a generous tip.

As he did so, he was astonished to see that moss was growing on the steps up to the front door.

Several of the windows were cracked and broken.

The door was open and as the Post-Chaise drove away the Earl walked into the hall.

It was then he stood as if he were shocked into immobility.

The hall, which he remembered as being particularly fine, was dirty and undusted.

There were ashes in the huge fireplace and an atmosphere of neglect which he thought must be part of his imagination.

There appeared to be no one about.

He remembered only too well there were always two liveried footmen on duty.

The Butler was always within call.

Finally he found his way to the Kitchen.

It was there from Marlow and Mrs. Marlow, who had been Butler and Cook since he was born, that he learned the truth.

From the moment he had left for India and his Uncle had taken over, Basil Burne had started to economise on everything.

He dismissed most of the staff, not only in the house but on the Estate.

"Us couldn't believe it, Master Michael," Mrs. Marlow said in a tearful voice, "and I kept thinking you'd come back from India and stop what that awful man was a-doing."

What that wicked man was doing, the Earl was to discover, was to take every penny that he possessed and put it in his name.

8

Holding Power of Attorney, Basil Burne had sold every share that his nephew owned.

He also sold everything in the Castle that was not entailed on to succeeding Earls.

Fortunately there was not a great deal not entailed.

But things which had belonged to his Mother had gone, and his Father's collection of snuff-boxes of which he had been exceedingly proud.

Early next morning, after a sleepless night, the Earl drove into Oxford to see his Father's Solicitors.

It had not been a fast journey.

There were only two horses left in the Stable, which had been kept by his Uncle for him to use, up to the last minute before he disappeared.

They were getting on in age and would travel only at a pace which suited them.

Single-handed the Marlows had looked after Basil Burne as best they could.

He told them bluntly they could stay with him and he would provide their board and lodging but they would have no wages.

"No wages!" the Earl exclaimed in horror.

"What could us do, My Lord?" Marlow asked. "If we left, it meant th' Workhouse."

"I cried and cried and pleaded with him," Mrs. Marlow joined in, "but he wouldn't listen. There were no one us could turn to for help."

"What did the Vicar have to say to all this?" the Earl asked.

"Oh, he left a year after Your Lordship went to India," Marlow replied. "Mr. Basil told him he wouldn't pay his stipend, so there be nothing he could do but go."

"So you mean the Church is closed."

"Someone comes from the other Parishes about once a month. Otherwise th' Vicarage be shut up, and I'm not sure who has the key of th' Church."

9

When the Earl confronted his Father's Solicitors, he had difficulty in choosing his words because he was so angry.

They should at least have written to tell him what was occurring.

The Solicitor facing him across the desk was an elderly man who, he learnt, had at first been entirely hoodwinked by his Uncle.

"He told me, My Lord, that things were difficult on the Stock Exchange," the Solicitor said, "and a great number of your Father's investments had fallen in value. So he thought it only right he should economise."

"Do you realise," the Earl asked angrily, "that the Pensioners have not been paid for three weeks, and before that they were getting only a pittance? I gather they are now on the verge of starvation."

"I did not know that, My Lord," the Solicitor replied. "Of course when the news came through that the Viceroy had been murdered, your Uncle would have expected that Your Lordship would come home."

"So he then took everything that he had not taken already," the Earl said sharply. "The servants tell me he has gone to America."

"If that is true," the Solicitor answered, "it will be very difficult to get hold of him. America is a very large country, and it would cost Your Lordship a great deal of money to bring a case against him."

"Which, as you are well aware," the Earl retorted, "I have not got."

As he drove back to the Castle, he wondered despairingly what he could do.

He had travelled home comfortably and had had a number of things to pay for in India before he left.

He had taken only a little money with him when he went out in the first place.

He then relied on his salary for what he required.

The Viceroy had been very particular in not letting his young ADC's run up debts.

He made it possible for them to have ample pocket-money while everything else, more or less, was provided for them.

The Earl realised now that he had nothing in the Bank, and his entire fortune, if that was the right word for it, consisted of under twenty pounds.

He had intended to cash a cheque at his Bank in London.

However, in the end he had just boarded the first train which would bring him back to the Castle.

"What am I to do? What the Devil am I to do?" he asked himself over and over again.

He knew frantically that he had to do something!

Then suddenly he felt as if the man he had loved and admired so much was guiding him.

"There must be someone," he told himself, "from whom I can borrow enough to at least keep my people from starving."

He had not missed, as he drove through the village, that the cottages all needed the thatch on their roofs to be repaired.

Windows were broken, gates were falling down.

It was obvious that not a spot of paint had been applied in the four years he had been away.

He remembered that in his Father's day the village had been one of the prettiest in the whole County.

People who had come to look at the Castle always admired the village too.

Now the only word to describe the situation was "appalling."

"I *must* have money," the Earl said, and it was a cry for help.

It was then he knew the answer.

Adjoining his Estate was that of Lord Frazer.

He was an enormously rich man whose Father had made a fortune in shipping.

He had come down from the north because he wished his son, who had been to Oxford, to get to know the right people.

The present Lord Frazer had quarrelled with his neighbour, the Tenth Earl of Rayburne, over a wood.

It was a very fine wood on the boundary between the two Estates.

The Earl of Rayburne, Michael's Father, had said that without question it belonged to him and always had.

Lord Frazer had contested this by producing an ancient map.

It depicted the wood as belonging to what was now the Frazer Estate.

The two old gentlemen fought fiercely for what they each believed to be their rights.

Shortly before his death, his Father had told him he was still getting rude letters from Lord Frazer, complaining that their gamekeepers had been in Monks Wood, interfering with his game.

"His game indeed!" the Earl had exclaimed. "I have never heard such impertinence! Those pheasants have been ours since the Thirteenth Century, and no amount of maps will convince me that I am wrong."

When Michael left for India, he had forgotten about Monks Wood.

Now he thought that if he agreed to let Lord Frazer take it once and for all as part of his Estate, he might lend him enough money to get his own land back to normal.

He had no idea what it would cost.

At least his experience in India with the Viceroy had taught him how to make fertile an area of land that was growing nothing.

Natives who had little knowledge of farming were shown how to produce crops and carry livestock.

The means by which the Viceroy had succeeded in the famine areas made him feel that he could do the same.

After all, the Rayburne Estate was not as large as India.

The Earl, therefore, told the old groom, who was driving him, to proceed to Watton Hall.

Wicks, who had been with his Father for over twenty years, said with the familiarity of an old servant:

"Yer Lordship won't get no change out of th' Master of Watton Hall. He's been a-fighting against us ever since he come there."

"I know that," the Earl said, "but I have an idea that might tempt him."

He thought that Wicks knew what he meant, but he did not comment.

He had learned how the servants had managed to keep alive after his Uncle had gone.

There were a few vegetables from the garden because the old gardener had remained in his cottage, having nowhere else to go.

They snared rabbits and even managed to shoot a wild duck or two on the lake.

"The Swans flew away a long time ago," he had been told, "after Mr. Burne refused to let us feed them."

Everything the Earl heard about his Uncle made him hate him more.

Yet Basil Burne was safely on the other side of the Atlantic.

The Earl doubted that he would be in the slightest perturbed by what anyone felt about him in the land he had left.

The only thing that mattered, the Earl knew, was to get enough money so that the Pensioners and children in the village would not starve.

Those who were still working on the land had received no wages since his Uncle had guessed he would be returning from India.

The Earl kept on turning over and over in his mind how shocking it all was.

While he had been so happy in India, he had no idea that his people were suffering, his fields were growing weeds, and his Castle was, day by day, becoming more dilapidated.

The horses turned in at the drive up to Watton Hall.

It was infuriating to see how well-kept everything looked.

The two lodges had obviously been recently painted, as had the iron gates with their gold tips.

It would be ridiculous to say that Watton Hall in any way rivalled the Castle.

Yet it was a prepossessing house, large and in its own way impressive.

It had been built in the Georgian style early in the reign of Queen Victoria.

As the horses drew up outside the porticoed front door, the Earl could not help feeling his appearance would be a great surprise to Lord Frazer.

He did not feel nervous, only slightly uncomfortable.

Then he remembered how his relative, the Viceroy, had always won everyone over to his side.

It was by what the Ladies in the Hill Stations called his magnetism and charisma.

He had, the Earl remembered, a quite deliberate way of speaking.

Those who met him found him easy-going and informal.

At the same time, he had a dignity which made it impossible for anyone to be unduly familiar.

The Earl remembered, too, that those who worked for him loved him both for his kindness and for his efficiency.

Surely, he thought, with Lord Mayo to guide him, he could get help from anyone, even from Lord Frazer!

The Butler, who was very smart, and the two footmen in the hall, looked at him with surprise.

He gave one of them his hat.

Then he followed the Butler down a wide passage into what he thought would be either the Library or Lord Frazer's Study.

It turned out to be the latter.

The owner of Watton Hall was sitting at a most impressive desk.

The inkpot, the pen-holder, and the candlestick with which to seal the letters were all made of solid gold.

"Th' Earl of Rayburne to see you, My Lord," the Butler announced in a stentorian voice.

Lord Frazer looked up in surprise.

Then he rose slowly to his feet as the Earl walked towards him.

As they shook hands, Lord Frazer said:

"I thought you would return from India after I heard the Viceroy had been murdered."

"I returned home immediately," the Earl replied, "and I have come to you, My Lord, for help."

He thought Lord Frazer raised his eyebrows.

At the same time, there was a glint of satisfaction in his eyes.

He indicated a chair in front of the fireplace.

As the Earl sat down, Lord Frazer seated himself in one beside it.

"I thought," he said as if he were deliberately choosing his words, "you would be surprised at what you found when you returned."

"I was not just surprised," the Earl said, "but horrified and appalled. How could any man, especially one who bears our family name, behave in such a shocking manner?"

"Your Uncle was greedy," Lord Frazer said, "and when I heard what was happening, I was surprised that no one communicated with you."

"That has not surprised me," the Earl said. "I understand my Uncle told my people they were my orders as well as his, and they therefore accepted there was nothing they could do."

"I heard he had gone to America," Lord Frazer remarked.

"That is what my Solicitors have just confirmed, and I have also discovered that he has taken every penny that I possessed with him."

"I thought that is what he would do," Lord Frazer remarked.

The Earl wanted to say he thought in that case he might have taken it upon himself to communicate with him.

However, he thought it wiser not to say so.

Instead, he said:

"I have come to you as my nearest neighbour to ask for your understanding and help."

He thought, as Lord Frazer did not say anything, that perhaps he was not as hostile as he had expected.

He went on quickly:

"I possess nothing at the moment that I can offer you except Monks Wood, which has always been a contested property between you and my Father."

He paused a moment and then continued:

"All I can say is that if you will trust me and lend me enough money to keep my people from starving and to get the farms working again, I will promise on my word of honour to pay back everything you have given me as speedily as is possible."

The Earl hoped as he spoke that he sounded convincingly trustworthy.

He hoped even more, since it was by no means a good business proposition, that Lord Frazer would be generous.

There was silence, and then Lord Frazer said:

"Have you any idea how much you need?"

16

"As much as you can possibly lend me," the Earl replied. "The Pensioners have been given no money for the last month. They were also down to half what my Father allowed them in his time."

His voice sharpened as he went on:

"Young men have been thrown off the land so that nothing has been cultivated. Some of them have left the village altogether to look for work, and the rest are just surviving on what they can poach in the woods, since there are no stags left in the Park."

"I heard they were killing them," Lord Frazer said. "But as they were not fed either, they were not very fat."

The Earl pressed his lips together.

He could not help noticing there was almost a triumphant sound in Lord Frazer's voice.

He could understand Lord Frazer was glad this was happening to a family who had opposed him for so long.

"I expect you know already," the Earl continued, "that the Castle has not been properly kept up since I have been away and, because most of the servants were sacked, it has not even been kept clean."

"I heard that," Lord Frazer murmured.

"Horses have also been sold out of the Stables. As you doubtless remember, my Father was proud of the horseflesh he possessed."

The Earl thought there was a glint of satisfaction in Lord Frazer's eyes.

"If you will not help me," he went on, "I must go back to London and beg from my friends whom I have not seen for four years."

He paused to say more quietly:

"I felt, My Lord, as our Estates march with each other, you would understand better than anyone else the predicament in which I find myself."

"Of course I understand," Lord Frazer replied. "Your Uncle's behaviour since you left has been the talk of the County."

The Earl had not realised this, and he frowned.

He thought, however, it would not help matters to comment.

"I suppose you could go cap in hand to our neighbours," Lord Frazer continued, "like the Lord Lieutenant who is known as one of the meanest men in Oxfordshire. When he attends Church, his contribution is not worthy of the seat on which he sits."

The Earl remembered this and he smiled.

"There is also Sir William Forrester," Lord Frazer continued, "who, I believe, has fallen on hard times because of his son's extravagance at the gambling tables. He is not likely to be open-handed to the young at this particular moment."

The Earl tried to think of someone who was known as being generous.

It was not a question he had asked before he went to India.

He had accepted people as they were, and had not been concerned with their bank-balance.

There was silence until at last he said pleadingly:

"Please, My Lord, help me if you can. It is not a question of me alone. The people who are at your gates as well as mine are on the verge of starvation."

Lord Frazer rose to his feet and stood with his back to the fireplace.

He was not a tall man, yet for the moment he reminded the Earl of Mount Harriet.

He and the Viceroy had climbed to the top and that was what he had to do now!

For his people's sake he must not fail.

Although it went against the grain to crawl, he kept seeing the faces of the children as he passed through the village.

They looked thin and pale.

He tried to pretend that it was not as bad as the

*18*

famine-stricken places he and the Viceroy had visited in India.

Yet it was bad enough for him to know that not only the old people were suffering but so were the children.

It was something that could not be allowed to continue.

He had to save them, however much he had to humiliate himself to do so.

With an effort, because it went against every grain in his body, he said:

"Please help me, My Lord, I am desperate, absolutely desperate. If you refuse, I can think of no one to whom I can turn."

His voice seemed to ring out, and he knew it came from the very depth of his being.

He had to save his own people, the people who had served his Father and Mother, as their parents had served his Grand-parents.

He had to save the Castle, the land, and eventually himself.

Lord Frazer did not answer.

He merely walked across to his desk and, opening a drawer, drew out a map.

He put it down on the carpet in front of the Earl.

He saw with surprise that it was a large and comprehensive map which covered the two Estates.

Both his own, which was very much larger, and, on the right-hand side, Watton Hall, with the two thousand acres which surrounded it, were featured.

The Earl had never seen it before, and he thought with surprise that Lord Frazer must have had it drawn recently.

He was sure of that when he saw it included cottages which had been built just before he went to India.

"I had this done a little while ago," Lord Frazer said, "because I thought it would be interesting to see the comparison between our two estates. As you see, Monks Wood separates us, and remains, of course, the bone of contention it has always been."

"That is why I have offered it to you," the Earl answered, "because I have nothing else that is not entailed on the son I shall never be able to afford."

He spoke bitterly. At the same time he despised himself for pleading with Lord Frazer.

He was obviously delighted that for the first time since he had lived at Watton Hall he had in his power a neighbour whose Father had proved so stubborn.

Once again the Earl thought of how the Viceroy would have handled this situation.

He knew that he would have used his charm, and at the same time, without losing his dignity, his friendliness.

The Earl said:

"Perhaps, My Lord, we can do something together. Not only in this emergency but in the future."

"That is exactly what I was thinking," Lord Frazer replied, "and what I have in mind is something which I actually thought of some years ago."

"What is that?" the Earl enquired.

"It was that our two Estates, which we know cover eight thousand acres, should be joined."

"Joined!" the Earl repeated.

He thought he was speaking rather stupidly.

His Father would no more have joined his land with that of Lord Frazer than fly over the moon.

He disliked the man and was determined that he should not get his way over Monks Wood.

Nevertheless Monks Wood would feed the Pensioners and save the children from starving.

He was, therefore, himself prepared to give it to Lord Frazer without bothering about it again.

"Now, what I will do," Lord Frazer said slowly, speaking as if he must emphasise every word, "is to give you twenty-five thousand pounds so that you can start to clean up the mess your Uncle has left behind."

The Earl stiffened in astonishment, then he gasped.

He thought at first he had not heard right what Lord Frazer had said.

His Lordship went on:

"When that is spent, and you will find that you need every penny of it, there will be the same amount to follow when you ask for it."

"I cannot begin—" the Earl began.

Lord Frazer held up his hand.

"My gift," he said, "is offered with one condition— that you marry my daughter."

## chapter two

FOR a moment the Earl thought he could not have heard right.

Then in a voice which did not sound like his own he exclaimed:

"Marry your daughter!"

"That is what I said," Lord Frazer replied, "and I think it is an excellent idea. Nothing could be more convenient for you than to have our two Estates joined together."

The Earl drew in his breath because he found it hard to think.

He had had no intention of marrying for many years yet, least of all a young girl.

The young girls he had met he had found extremely boring.

When he was in India he had spent his time in a very different manner.

The Ladies in the Hill Stations were alluring but inevitably already married.

They had left their husbands on the plains when they went up to Simla and hoped they would not be asked too many awkward questions on their return.

The Hill Stations were the scene of many love affairs, but they were transient and extremely discreet.

The Earl would not have been human if he had not accepted the favours he was offered.

In fact, if he was not dashing somewhere with the Viceroy, he was always in the company of some soft and gentle but very attractive woman.

He had known that some day he would have to marry to have an heir.

He was, however, only twenty-seven, and he thought it would not be a serious problem for at least ten years.

To be confronted now with marriage, not with someone he loved or who even just attracted him but with a young woman he had never seen, was horrifying.

It was worse because he disliked Lord Frazer no less than his Father had.

He could imagine any daughter he produced would make their marriage a disaster from the moment it took place.

Without quite realising what he was doing, he rose to his feet and walked to the window.

He looked out on a perfect garden.

The lawns were as smooth as velvet, the flowers in the beds seemed almost to stand to attention, and the whole aspect was one that could be achieved only by a multitude of gardeners.

'That,' he thought bitterly, 'is what money can do!'

It had taken only one glance at the gardens round the Castle for him to realise they had been completely neglected.

In fact, they must have run wild from the moment he had set off for India.

He had learned from Marlow that all the gardeners also had been sacked.

Only Cosnat, the head-gardener, was left, who, having nowhere else to go, had stayed on because he too was afraid of the Workhouse.

The Earl had the idea, as he stood there thinking, that Lord Frazer was regarding his back with amusement.

He was well aware that he had thrown a bombshell and had led up to it, the Earl thought, in a way which was somehow despicable.

There was a long silence.

Then Lord Frazer said:

"Of course you can carry on as you are, but I think you will find it a hard and stony road."

It was with difficulty the Earl did not turn round and reply that however stony it might be, it was what he preferred to being tied to someone.

Then he found himself once again asking the Viceroy what he should do.

Instead of the handsome, clean-shaven face that he had admired, he could see the children in the village, their pinched faces, their pale cheeks, before him.

They were not running about and playing, but just sitting limply by the roadside or propped against a broken gate of their cottage.

He remembered how much the children of India had meant to Mayo and how deeply he loved his own.

The Viceroy's little son Terence was always allowed to help his Father put on his Star.

He would sit on his dressing-table to do it.

Because the Viceroy was so pressed for time, he often did business with his colleagues in his dressing-room while he was changing.

When Terence was there he would say if the discussion was confidential:

"Why, Terry-boy, you are my confidant, are you not? You are quite discreet too, aren't you?"

The Earl could almost see now little Terence's face light up as he smiled at his Father.

Sometimes he would put his arms round his neck and kiss him.

If that was what a child meant to the man he had admired and emulated, how could he allow other children to starve?

Whatever the sacrifice on his part, he had to make it.

With a superhuman effort he turned round and said to Lord Frazer:

"Of course I would like to meet your daughter and find out if she will accept an empty-handed Bridegroom."

"There is no question of that," Lord Frazer answered sharply. "Today is Tuesday. You can be married on Thursday morning at the Church at which I have appointed the Vicar. That will give your people time to buy food on Friday to keep them from starving over the weekend."

The Earl stared at him.

"I cannot quite see the reason," he said, "for such haste. Of course I must talk to your daughter before we are married."

Lord Frazer sat down at his writing-desk.

"You do things my way, young man," he said, "or find someone else to finance you."

"I can hardly think you mean that," the Earl protested.

"I mean every word of it," Lord Frazer replied. "You will marry my daughter on Thursday morning, and when you sign the Register I will hand you a cheque."

He paused a moment and then went on sternly:

"Until then you must feed yourself and your people with what they can find on your land, which I can assure you is very little."

The way he spoke was so offensive that the Earl felt like hitting him.

But he thought of Mayo's twinkling eyes and the way he would smile with a twist to his lips when someone behaved badly.

"If that is your last word, My Lord," he said, "then you know as well as I do that I have to accept it. I can only say it is a strange way of getting married which I should imagine any young woman would resent."

"My daughter does as she is told," Lord Frazer said. "If you take my advice, you will make your wife do the same. A man must be Master in his own house."

The Earl longed to say that while he agreed with that in principle, there was no need to be so aggressive or so unpleasant about it.

He knew despairingly there was nothing he could say or do at the moment. He was completely in Lord Frazer's power and he could not see any way of escape.

It was like a yawning cavity opening in front of him.

He had the feeling that once he had stepped into it, he would never be able to escape.

That indeed was the truth.

If he married Lord Frazer's daughter, she would be his wife and, as the Marriage Ceremony said:

" 'Til death us do part."

Every instinct in his body cried out against it.

Although he would never admit it even to himself, he was a romantic.

His Father and Mother had fallen in love with each other at first sight.

They had been extremely happy and he hoped that was what would happen to him.

When he was ready for marriage, he told himself in a dreamlike fantasy, he would meet a beautiful woman perhaps at a Ball or maybe out hunting.

When he looked into her eyes he would know this was the one he had been searching for and until that moment had failed to find.

She naturally would feel the same about him.

Without being conceited, the Earl was confident there would be no difficulty about that.

He was only too well aware that when he entered a room there was invariably a subtle invitation in the eyes looking at him.

When he talked to the woman in question there would be a provocative little pout to her lips.

Her long and slender fingers would reach out to touch his arm.

He had never yet been attracted to a woman who was not eager to receive his advances.

In fact, sometimes he thought a little cynically that they were ready to fall into his arms before he asked their name.

How, then, could he marry a girl whom he had never even seen and who had never seen him?

How could she possibly be attracted to a man to whom she had been sold simply because he had a title and a larger Estate than her Father's.

The Earl had learned to face facts.

He knew only too well that ambitious Mothers looked on him as very acceptable *parti* for their daughters.

As it was, he knew that Lord Frazer would not be so keen on having him as a son-in-law if he were not of such Social importance.

Even though he was penniless, he was the owner of one of the most beautiful and legendary Castles in the country.

"Why do I have to do this? Why?" he asked.

Then once again he saw the children in the village getting thinner and paler.

He had calculated as he was returning from the Solicitor's Office the time when his Uncle had started to pack up his stolen belongings.

It would have been the moment he heard of the Viceroy's death.

This meant his people had endured over a month of starvation.

His Solicitors had told him that his Uncle had left just over two weeks after the newspapers were filled with the story of the Viceroy's assassination.

The Earl assumed that Basil Burne had spent those weeks in selling shares and closing the bank accounts.

He also sold frantically every available object he had not sold already.

Now with the money he would receive from Lord Frazer he could at least buy back some of the treasures which had belonged to his Mother.

But what had to come first was the restoration not only of the Castle, but the villages.

He was well aware that the village at his gate, which was the largest, was not the only place where he had Pensioners.

There were many others, too, who in the past had been employed on the farms of the Estate.

The more he thought about it, the more he was quite certain that he would need every penny of the twenty-five thousand Lord Frazer was dangling in front of him.

He knew, as he did not speak, Lord Frazer was waiting for his reply, confident that he had already won the contest.

There was no chance whatever of his victim refusing to comply with the terms he had offered.

With a dignity which was worthy of Mayo himself, the Earl turned round.

"I accept your proposition, My Lord," he said, "and I can only thank you for helping me out in an extremely difficult and unforeseen situation."

He did not look at Lord Frazer as he spoke.

He could not bear to see the expression of satisfaction in his eyes.

Instead, he said:

29

"Now I must go home and tell my people what the situation is."

He paused before he added:

"I suppose there will be none of the usual festivities at my wedding with your daughter?"

"None!" Lord Frazer said sharply. "I see no point in our neighbours in the County learning what has happened."

The Earl looked surprised, and Lord Frazer went on:

"They doubtless know of the scandalous way in which your Uncle has behaved, and I see no reason for them to be surprised under the circumstances that you marry my daughter so that she can help you reconstruct your Castle and your property."

The Earl thought Lord Frazer was certainly deceiving himself.

No one would think he had married Lord Frazer's daughter in such indecent haste unless it was to obtain her Father's money.

However, what people did or did not say was not of particular importance.

He knew how worried his Father would have been.

He would certainly have objected to his marrying Lord Frazer's daughter however temptingly he was bribed to do so.

"But what else can I do?" he asked himself as he drove away from Watton Hall.

He knew he had been forced into submission.

It was something he would no doubt deeply regret for the rest of his life.

He had two more days of freedom, two days in which he had the chance, if he were brave enough to take it, to tell Lord Frazer he would manage without him.

But as he entered the village, he saw the first thatched roof that was in bad repair and was obviously letting in the rain.

He knew then he had to steel himself.

"Go to the *'Fox and Geese,'* " he said to Wicks.

This was a little further on, a pretty black and white Public House which stood on the village green.

It was the favourite haunt, the Earl knew, of every man in the neighbourhood.

They seldom came off the fields without popping in to see Joe Higgins, although they did not always buy a glass of ale.

The village green was just as he remembered it, except there were no ducks on the pond.

The Earl thought that they must have made a meal for some hungry Villagers.

Seated outside the Public House on the wooden benches in front of which was a trestle-table, were three old men.

There were no mugs in front of them, nor were they smoking.

The Earl was sure they went there purely out of habit.

It was some consolation to know the *'Fox and Geese'* was still standing.

As Wicks drew up the horses, they turned their heads to look at the Earl as he stepped out of the carriage.

But they did not move.

Nor did they smile or touch their forelocks as they would have in the past.

The Earl did not speak to them.

He walked inside and into the bar, where he was sure he would find Joe Higgins.

He was not mistaken, but Joe was not busy with bottles and barrels as he usually had been.

He was just sitting on the stool he had always sat on, looking disconsolate.

"I have come home, Joe," the Earl said quietly.

"So Oi heard," Joe replied without moving. "And Oi suppose yer know what's happened to us."

"I have heard," the Earl said. "I have come to you because I want your help."

31

"Help!" Joe Higgins exclaimed. "How can Oi or any-one else help ye? There's not a soul in th' village who ain't as hungry as a hunter, but there be nowt to eat and nowt to drink. Oi never thinks in all me life Oi'd see anything like it."

"Nor did I," the Earl agreed, "and that is why I have to do something about it."

"And what can ye do?" Joe asked. "Us all knows as yer Uncle, may th' Devil take him, has gone across th' sea with everything yer possesses. While us all dies to-gether."

"You are not going to die," the Earl said firmly. "But I need your help—"

Before he could finish the second one of Joe's sons, a young man of just over twenty, came in the door at the back of the bar.

He was holding up a rabbit and exclaimed:

"Look what Oi've caught! Us'll not go hungry tonight at any rate."

Then, as he looked towards his Father, he saw the Earl.

Instinctively he put the rabbit he had obviously snared in the Park behind his back.

"Oi didna' k-know Yer L-Lordship were here," he stammered.

"It is all right, Colin," the Earl said, remembering the boy's name with an effort. "You can have everything you can snare on my land with my blessing. But now I want you to do something for me."

"What be that?" Colin enquired somewhat suspi-ciously.

"I want you to ask everyone in the village to come here immediately," the Earl said. "I want to explain to them what I am planning for the future. So get everyone you can, and quickly!"

Colin looked at the Earl in surprise, then at his Father.

"Get on with it!" Joe growled.

There was another boy with Colin of about the same age.

They put down the snare and the dead rabbit and they hurried across the green into the main street.

The Earl seated himself on one of the wooden stools beside the bar.

"If yer want something to eat," Joe said after a moment, "Oi haven't got it. When things got bad they comes in to drown their sorrows. But when 'twas a question of a bite or a drink, an' a mighty small bite at that, they thinks o' their stommach rather than their thirst."

"I can understand that," the Earl said, "but I promise you, Joe, that is not going to continue. And if you have a glass of water, I should be grateful for it."

He would have liked something very much stronger after the shock he had just experienced.

Slowly Joe moved to the back of the bar.

There was the sound of him moving about clinking bottles which the Earl was sure were empty.

Then he came back with a small glass of Cider.

"Oi were keeping this for meself," he said, "but now Oi thinks of it, Oi suppose, M'Lord, yer need be greater than mine."

The Earl realised he had addressed him formally for the first time.

That meant his anger and resentment were melting a little.

Joe had a warm and friendly welcome for anyone who entered the Public House and was a character well known for miles around.

"Cheerful Joe" he used to be called.

He had been fat and jolly in a hearty way which everyone appreciated.

He little resembled that now.

He now looked like an old man with round shoulders and heavy lines on his sad face.

He was bald except for a few white hairs.

"I am very grateful," the Earl said, "and I will pay for it a little later when I have spoken to the Villagers."

"Oi supposes they'll come out of curiosity," Joe said. "But Oi expects yer understand they're hating Yer Lordship for leaving 'em in this mess. If yer Uncle hadn't skipped it, they'd 'ave torn him limb from limb."

The Earl did not answer, he merely sipped the homemade Cider.

He could hear the sound of voices outside.

It gradually went on, increasing while he and Joe sat in silence, listening.

It was half-an-hour later when Colin opened the door to say:

"They be all here 'cept 'em as can't walk."

"Thank you, Colin," the Earl said. "I want you and your friend to listen to what I have to say because it concerns you both."

Colin looked surprised as he answered:

"We'll do that, Yer Lordship."

The Earl went out through the door.

As he had expected, there was a large number of the Villagers waiting for him.

Some of the older women had dragged some more benches from the side of the Inn so that they could sit down.

The younger women were sitting on the grass and most of the men were standing.

When the Earl appeared, there was complete and absolute silence.

They just stared at him.

He knew they were wondering what he would say and if they could tell him the horrors he had inflicted on them.

There was a stone mounting-block at the side of the door which had been there for years.

The Earl got up on it.

It was only about two feet high, but it made it possible for everyone to see him clearly.

Speaking in a loud, clear, but not too quick manner which he had learnt from the Viceroy, he said:

"I hoped when I was on my way back from India that it would be a happy and exciting occasion to meet you, my people, again. Instead, you know what has happened and the appalling condition in which I found both my home and my property."

"What yer going t' do 'bout it?" a man shouted from the back.

"That is just what I am going to tell you," the Earl replied. "I have asked you to come here because I have just come from the Solicitors, where I learnt that my Uncle, whom I trusted, has taken with him to America every penny that I inherited from my Father."

"Then wot about us?" another man shouted.

"I have been thinking about you all the way back from Oxford. So I stopped to call on Lord Frazer at Watton Hall."

When the Earl said this, he was aware of surprise on the faces of the Villagers.

They knew only too well of the animosity which had always existed between the two Estates.

"Now," the Earl said, "I am going to take you into my confidence and trust you, because you have all known me since I was a small boy, not to speak of it outside our village. If we have to fight battles to save ourselves, there is no reason why other people should know our secrets or criticise what we have done."

He realised the women appreciated this, and he went on:

"I have persuaded Lord Frazer to lend me—and I am determined to return it because it is a loan and not a gift—enough money for us together to restore the Rayburne Estate to what it was in my Father's time."

"If yer got that from old man Frazer, Oi donna believe it," one of the listeners remarked.

"It is true," the Earl said," "and you will not be surprised to hear that I offered him Monks Wood."

There was a faint smile on one or two faces.

"What I have promised," the Earl continued, "is to marry Miss Ansella Frazer on Thursday."

There was an audible gasp from the older women sitting on the benches.

The younger ones on the grass sat up abruptly.

"Marry Lord Frazer's daughter?" one of the older women asked. "Yer Father'd turn in 'is grave."

"I think he would understand," the Earl replied, "that I cannot allow you to go on suffering as you are suffering now. Therefore on Thursday afternoon following the Marriage Ceremony in the morning, everyone here who has ever been employed by me will go back to work."

He stopped speaking for a moment to allow the fact to be absorbed by his audience before he went on:

"They will receive three month's wages on Friday morning. Or, if I can manage it, on the afternoon of my wedding."

Now there was a cry which was not very loud but at the same time extremely moving.

"The Pensioners will receive the same," the Earl went on, "three months of the full pension they had when my Father was alive, and this will be increased again as soon as it is possible."

"Oi don't believe it," one old woman said. "Oi must be dreaming. In fact, Oi knows Oi am."

Her voice broke and there were tears running down her cheeks.

"Now, what I need up at the house," the Earl continued, "are four footmen like Marlow always had in the past. I am sure Colin would like to be one of them."

"Oi'd like that, M'Lord," Colin said, "and so would m' friend Cyril."

"Come and see Marlow as soon as I leave here," the Earl said. "I shall also need two able women in the Kitchen to help Mrs. Marlow, and two scullions. I think that was what my Father always had."

"Aye, it were," one woman said, "and it'll be like old times to be helpin' Mrs. Marlow again."

"And I understand," the Earl continued, "that Mrs. Shepherd, my Housekeeper, is somewhere in the village, but I do not see her here."

" 'Er says as it'd hurt 'er too much to see yer," Colin explained.

"Tell her I will send a carriage for her tomorrow morning," the Earl said, "and I want three or four house-maids immediately to help her clean up the Castle which it badly needs."

The younger girls started murmuring amongst themselves as to who should apply.

The Earl held up his hand for silence.

"I have not quite finished," he said. "I am being completely honest with you when I tell you that the only ready money I possess is just under twenty pounds and I will not have any more until after my marriage."

There was a murmur at this, but he went on:

"What I intend to do is to keep a few pounds for the Marlows to supply food for me and anyone who starts tomorrow to work in the Castle. The fifteen pounds which is left I am giving to Joe to buy some food for you all in the meantime and distribute it as he thinks best."

Again there was a gasp.

Then they cheered.

Their voices rose and at the same time many of them were trembling with tears.

"I am sure Joe will know better than I do what to do," the Earl said. "I should think if you buy a heifer from one of Lord Frazer's farms it will be fat enough to provide everyone in the village with a good meal before they receive their wages."

37

The voices rose, but again he held up his hand.

"For those who are too old or who have no wish to go on the land," he said, "there is work to be done in the village. I want every cottage rethatched, repainted, and repaired."

There was a breathless cheer, and he continued:

"I know there are carpenters and painters amongst you. So will you get busy as soon as it is possible to obtain the materials, the paint, and everything else you require. I want to go back to the days when people came to admire Rayburne Castle and to enthuse over the prettiest village in the whole County."

He paused while they cheered again, then added:

"As I said when I started, all this can be done only with your help. So please, because you loved my Father and Mother and have always been kind to me, forget the horrors that have been inflicted on you by my Uncle and let us be a happy family again as we were in the past."

It was then they began really cheering.

The men waved their caps and their arms and the women their handkerchiefs.

The Earl went round to shake hands with everyone.

He kissed the cheeks of some of the older women and they loved him for it.

When he had handed the fifteen pounds he had in his pocket to Joe, the old man said:

"Oi never thought Oi'd see the day when Oi would thank God on me knees for yer, Master Michael, but that's what Oi'm a-doing now."

"Just go on praying for me," the Earl said. "I am going to need it."

As he drove back towards the Castle, he knew that was indeed the truth.

He was going to need every prayer and every good wish it was possible to be offered for him.

Then he looked up at the Castle.

The sun was now setting behind it with a golden glow.

He felt that any sacrifice was worthwhile if it would preserve something that mattered so much to him, just as it had mattered to his ancestors before him.

Then, as if all the Devils in hell were clawing at him, he found himself thinking of the wife he was forced to have.

She would doubtless be thick-set and heavy, and rather like her Father.

She would also never let him forget it was her Father's money which had saved him, her Father's money that was preventing the Castle from falling down, his people from starving, and his land from becoming a barren desert.

If she did not actually say it in words, he would know she was thinking it.

He thought there was nothing more degrading than being subservient to a woman who would despise him for his weakness as a man.

She would jeer at him because he had been forced to accept her as his wife.

He almost felt like running away, re-joining his Regiment, and trying to return to India.

Then he knew that was certainly something that the Viceroy would never have done.

Mayo had faced enormous difficulties when he first reached India.

Somehow he had managed to solve problems which seemed insoluble, to make friends where there was only enemies.

Wherever he went, people had learnt to think of him as a friend and someone they could trust.

As the Earl walked into the Castle he told himself that was what he had to try to achieve.

Although, he added, God knew, nothing could be more difficult.

He told the Marlows what had been arranged, and Mrs. Marlow burst into floods of tears.

"It be just like yer, Master Michael," she said, "to make us happy again. Yer always were a darling little boy, and the first thing I'll make for you when we have th' ingredients'll be yer gingerbread biscuits."

She could hardly say the words through her tears.

The Earl put his hand on her shoulder.

"You have always spoilt me, Mrs. Marlow," he said, "and I want you to spoil me again. It is not going to be easy having someone take my Mother's place."

"I knows that," Mrs. Marlow agreed, "and yet know that Marlow and I'll do everything us can. But Lord Frazer's daughter! What would yer dear Father say if he knew?"

"I think he would understand," the Earl replied for the second time.

He left the kitchen and went to his Father's room.

It was a Study where they had usually sat when they were alone because it was a cosy room.

Now it looked bare, dirty, and dusty.

The Earl saw that his Uncle had removed and presumably sold the decorative china on the mantelpiece which was not entailed.

Some pictures which his Father had bought of horses, which were considerably more valuable than the price he had paid for them, had also gone.

There were gaps in the bookcase which made the Earl suspicious.

They were First Editions.

Of course they were entailed with the books in the Library, but these too had been sold to fill his Uncle's pocket.

He sat down at his Father's desk and put his head in his hands.

He felt as if the problems which lay ahead were being repeated and repeated in his brain.

He could not escape from them.

The worst problem of all was that he must accept Lord Frazer's money and Lord Frazer's daughter.

He was well aware that it would take him years to pay back, as he intended to do, the twenty-five thousand pounds.

But every nerve in his body told him he would not accept it as a gift.

Somehow in some miraculous way he was determined to be able to tell Lord Frazer he did not want a further loan.

He would return the original loan he had accepted only because he had been desperate.

"How can I ever to that?" he asked himself.

He knew all too clearly that the one thing he could not return was his wife.

She would be there with him, day after day, year after year.

If they had children, he felt that somehow Lord Frazer would hold him even more firmly in a trap.

He was already irrevocably caught.

Because he could not bear to go on thinking of it, he left his Father's Study and walked along the corridor until he reached the old Castle itself.

There was a door into it and then the winding stone staircase which led up to the roof.

He climbed the steps as he had done so often when he was a small boy.

He opened the door at the top of the steps and went out onto the roof.

His first thought was that repairs were needed on the stone-work.

There were the remains of a dead pigeon lying in the centre of the Tower.

He picked it up by its leg and threw it over the far end.

The Castle had at one time been surrounded by a moat.

Most of this had been removed with the exception of a large pool at the far end.

When the rains came it became wider and bulged out on either side of the Tower.

At the moment it was not large, but the Earl knew it was very deep.

There were many legends of the battles between the Burnes and their enemies.

They would, the Earl had been told, throw their prisoners, tied up with ropes, into the moat, where they drowned.

He did not know whether this was true or not.

The Earl had believed it as a small boy.

He thought now that perhaps if his life with Lord Frazer's daughter was an utter fiasco, there was always the moat waiting for him.

Then he forced himself to laugh at his own fancy and his own dismal despair.

If the girl had been bullied by her Father, and there was no doubt Lord Frazer was a bully, then she would expect to be bullied by her husband.

He would be able to keep her in order.

He would prevent her from annoying him more than was absolutely necessary.

He turned away to look at the entrancing view which swept away over the fertile Oxfordshire land to a hazy horizon.

It was so beautiful, it seemed for the moment to wipe away the Earl's fears and depression.

Whatever else happened, no one could take this from him.

He was a part of it as he had been from the moment he was born.

The Castle was his and he would make it a place of defiance.

What had just happened would never occur again either for him or those who came after him.

It was almost as if he made a vow.

Then beneath his breath he murmured:

"So help me God!"

## *chapter three*

THE Earl woke from what had been a very restless sleep to awareness that it was his Wedding Day.

He thought that the sky should be dark and there should be fog over the land, instead of which the sun was shining and the birds were singing.

He got up slowly, feeling as if his legs would not carry him, and went to the window.

Already Cosnat had four men working in the garden and he himself had taken on a new lease of life.

The Earl understood how much it had hurt him to see the garden overgrown with weeds and broken panes of glass in the greenhouses.

The kitchen-garden, he learnt, had produced less and less that was edible.

Now Cosnat seemed almost like a young man as he ordered his assistants about.

The youths had hurried up from the village to be engaged to work in the garden.

The Earl had spent the previous day riding on one of the old horses as far as he could on the Estate.

He found, as expected, the farmers dejected and their wives in tears.

Because Basil Burne had advanced them no money for seed, there had been no crops.

When he had cut off every support for them, they had been obliged to eat their own sheep and cattle.

The Earl told them everything was to be changed.

He promised to let them have as much as he could to build up their farms.

They could hardly believe what they were hearing.

There would be a great amount of repairs to be done.

He said he would send them men from the village to repair the roofs and to make new chicken-houses.

By the time he had visited two farms, he found he had already spent a great deal of money.

At that rate it would not be long before he would be obliged to ask Lord Frazer for the second loan he had promised him.

Now the day of reckoning had come.

He felt as if he were walking into a fiery furnace.

His Father and Mother had been so happy together.

It had never occurred to him for one moment that he would marry for anything except love.

As he had never even flirted with young girls, the question of marriage had never arisen.

Now that the moment had come when he had to take a Bride, he felt his whole instinct rebelling against it.

Yet he was completely and absolutely committed.

He had given his word as a Gentleman and he could not go back on it.

Moreover, the satisfaction of seeing the happiness on the faces round him was a compensation in itself.

He knew that his own people were disappointed there were to be no Wedding Festivities such as had always taken place in the past.

That had meant two huge tents on the lawn and a sit-down supper with great barrels of beer.

There would be fireworks when it was dark which would reflect in the lake and be watched with wild excitement by the children.

He thought that was what he himself would arrange later.

But Lord Frazer would think it a waste of his money if it was used on amusing peasants rather than himself.

'I will manage something,' he determined.

He was certain it would cause an argument with his wife.

She would certainly come to him having been told by her Father to see that the money her husband was spending was not wasted.

Lord Frazer was known as a hard task-master and was disliked by most of the Villagers.

The Earl was quite certain that his wife would in no way take the place of his Mother.

He remembered how she had always called on people who were sick or old.

She attended the Christening of nearly every baby born in the village.

She was inevitably asked to be a Godmother and took a personal interest in the child from the moment it came into the world.

The Earl remembered letters she had received.

Boys and girls who had gone to work in other towns or parts of England had never forgotten her.

They had written home not only to their Mothers but also to "the Lady in the Castle" whom they loved.

How could he expect Lord Frazer's daughter to be anything like that?

The idea was laughable if it had not been so depressing.

He dressed himself as carefully as if he were going to a Wedding at St. George's in London.

He had attended one just before he had left for India.

The Prince and Princess of Wales had been present.

It had been one of the smartest Weddings and Receptions of the Season.

He had gone because the Bridegroom had been at Oxford with him.

He had fallen in love the moment he entered London Society with one of the prettiest and most eligible *débutantes*.

The Earl had been asked to be one of the Groomsmen.

He had shown a very distinguished company, whose names were all in Debrett, into their pews.

He had also attended the Bridegroom's Bachelor dinner three nights previously.

It had taken place in one of the smartest Restaurants in London, fortunately in a private room.

He had drunk a great deal, and the fifteen other young men present had laughed all through a delicious meal.

They had ended up by singing "The Eton Boating Song" because it was where most of them had been educated.

Then they staggered home in the early hours of the morning.

The Earl had had a headache the next day.

He decided that if and when he gave a Bachelor dinner, he would try to think of something original.

Those who were present would always remember it afterwards.

It was just a passing thought.

Yet something deep within himself made him think that so much drink and rather bawdy stories were not in keeping with a Wedding, not if a man loved the woman he was marrying so much that he felt he could not go on living without her.

He had not actually thought of that again.

But now it came to his mind.

Perhaps deep in his subconscious he had always been looking for the real love of which the poets had written.

Anyway, that was something that was not to be for him!

He took a last look at himself in the mirror to see that he was tidy.

He could not help thinking that his wife would not be able to find fault with his appearance.

So many women had told him that he looked like a Greek God that he began to believe it himself.

Now he laughed at his own conceit and thought that no one would mistake Lord Frazer's daughter for a Goddess from Mount Olympus.

He went downstairs.

When he reached the hall, only Marlow was there.

As he handed the Earl his top-hat, he said:

"I wants to give yer, M'Lord, me best wishes and those of everyone in the Castle. We all knows as Yer's a-doing this for us and we thanks yer for it."

The Earl was very touched.

He put his hand on Marlow's arm and said:

"There is nothing else I can do. But you know that my Father would not have approved."

"Indeed he wouldn't," Marlow agreed, "and I only hopes that wherever His Lordship be, he's not aware of what yer're having to do."

The Earl felt the same.

But there was nothing more he could say.

He walked out the front door and down the steps.

The two old horses were waiting for him.

He was determined on one thing, that he would at least have a few young and decent horses in the Stables as quickly as possible.

He would be able to ride them to relieve his feelings and also to escape from his wife.

They drove down the drive.

When they went out through the gates, which badly needed repair, he saw there were a number of Villagers waiting in the road.

He realised that as they could not come to the Wedding, they were waiting to wave and wish him good luck as he passed them.

Wicks was aware of this and deliberately drove slowly:

"Good luck!" "God bless ye!" "May ye be happy!"

The voices rang out and one or two children threw flowers into the open carriage.

The Earl raised his hat.

He could not help thinking that their wishes would not be answered.

There was no chance of his being anything but extremely unhappy.

When they passed the last dilapidated thatched cottage, Wicks pushed the horses.

They moved quickly down the twisting lane which led to Watton Hall.

It was a little time before they reached the boundary between the two Estates.

Then, of course, there was Monks Wood to pass.

The Earl looked at it and thought of how angry the quarrel about it had made his Father.

What must he feel now, when his only son was forced to marry the daughter of the man he had always considered his enemy?

They drove on and came to the village that lay outside the gates of Watton Hall.

Here the cottages were trim, neat, and newly painted.

The village Church was not so old, nor so historically interesting as the one on the Earl's Estate.

It was only a short distance from the two lodges and gold-tipped gates leading up to the Hall.

In fact, the Churchyard at the back of the Church was actually inside the Park.

The Earl was somewhat relieved to see there were no crowds outside the Church.

He had expected that the Villagers, who were all in Lord Frazer's service, would be clustered round the door.

They would want to see the Bride and Bridegroom when they arrived and to shower them with rice and rose petals when they left.

Then it struck him that Lord Frazer would not advertise that his daughter was being married to save the neighbouring Estate.

Therefore his people, unlike the Earl's, were unaware of what was happening.

Wicks drew the horses to a standstill.

The Earl stepped out.

There was no one to meet him at the church gate.

As he walked towards the door he heard the faint sound of an organ.

Taking off his hat, he walked in.

To his surprise, he found there was no one in the Church but the Vicar.

He was turning over the leaves of the Bible on the lectern.

When he saw the Earl he hurried down the aisle towards him.

He was an elderly man who seemed a little flustered.

He held out his hand, saying:

"Good morning, My Lord. I see you are punctual, and I do not think His Lordship will keep you waiting too long."

The Earl walked to the front pew on which he deposited his hat.

Then, as he stood somewhat irresolute in the aisle, the Vicar said:

"Is there any particular prayer, My Lord, you would like said on this auspicious occasion?"

"I shall be quite content with the ordinary Service," the Earl replied.

He was looking at the Altar on which he saw there was a small but not in any way impressive arrangement of white flowers.

He could also see a woman playing the organ, which was on the other side of the choir-stalls.

As if he were answering a question he had not been asked, the Vicar said:

"It is my wife, My Lord, who is playing for you. His Lordship was insistent that the Wedding was to be a very quiet one and therefore there will be no guests."

The Earl was surprised.

Then it occurred to him that Lord Frazer was being very clever about the Wedding.

He had forced his daughter on a man who did not want her.

That was something he had no wish for the outside world to know.

However, his daughter would have made an exceptionally good Social Marriage.

The Earls of Rayburne were acknowledged as one of the oldest and most distinguished families in the country.

The Earl thought cynically that Lord Frazer was hard and quite clever.

He wished to conceal from people in the County and his friends, if he had any, that this was an exceptional situation.

It was not something of which either he or the Bride-groom would be particularly proud.

The Vicar fidgeted for a moment.

Then, making the excuse that he wanted to get his Prayer-Book, he hurried away into the Vestry.

The Earl knew that he was embarrassed at what he thought was a very hole-in-the-corner Wedding.

He could, however, hardly criticise the man who paid his stipend.

The Earl sat down in the front pew.

Then, as the minutes ticked by, he knew that Lord Frazer was deliberately being late.

It was to make him feel worried in case he had changed his mind at the last moment and the money would not be forthcoming.

It was so unpleasant a thought that the Earl set his lips in a hard line.

His chin was very square as he waited and went on waiting.

The Vicar's wife came to the end of the piece she was playing.

She hurriedly turned back the pages of her music to start all over again.

The Earl drew his watch out of his vest-pocket and saw that his Bride was now nearly twenty minutes late.

As he looked at his watch, it struck him that was something he might have sold or pawned to obtain money.

It had been given to him on his twenty-first birthday by his Father and Mother and he had cherished it ever since.

It was something he would hate to part with.

If his Bride did not turn up as arranged, and the money was not forthcoming, it would have to go.

It would be only a small drop in the ocean of what was required.

He was beginning to count up what else was available, only to find, as he knew already, it was very little.

Then, at last, twenty-five minutes late, there was a sound of wheels outside the Church door.

The Vicar, who must have heard them too, came hurrying from the Vestry.

Lord Frazer came through the doorway of the Church.

The Earl rose from the pew to stand with his back to the aisle and facing the Altar.

This was the moment when he would see his future wife for the first time.

He felt a revulsion he could not control sweeping over him.

Lord Frazer's footsteps were very slow coming up the aisle.

It was as if he were deliberately prolonging the agony.

He knew that was what the Bridegroom would feel because of the Bride's late arrival.

They reached the steps to the Chancel.

Now, because he had to move forward, the Earl had his first glance at the woman he was to marry.

As her head was bent forwards, she looked even smaller in comparison with her Father.

She was wearing a Brussels lace veil over her face and the traditional orange blossom wreath.

It was impossible for the Earl to have any idea what she looked like.

Anyway, he had no wish to look at her.

He fixed his eyes on the Vicar, who immediately started the Marriage Service.

He did not read it very well.

The Earl thought it was because he was nervous of Lord Frazer.

He seemed without speaking to dominate not only the Church but the people in it.

They reached the point when the Vicar asked the Earl for a Wedding-ring and he produced his Mother's.

It was something he had no wish to give any woman.

He had, however, not had a chance of buying a ring before the Service took place.

Anyway, it would be a foolish waste of money when so much was demanded of the few pounds he had taken back to the Castle, having given the rest of what he owned to Joe Higgins.

54

He had suspected when he looked at the ring it would be far too small.

He expected his Bride to be a big woman because she was Lord Frazer's daughter.

The Vicar blessed the ring.

Then as he handed it back to the Earl, the Bride moved for the first time.

Her left hand came slowly from beneath her veil.

She held it out.

The Earl was then aware that she was trembling so violently that her hand seemed to move backwards and forwards in front of his eyes.

With some difficulty he managed to slip the ring onto her third finger.

It fitted and she moved her hand away quickly.

When the Bride and Bridegroom repeated their vows, the Earl was aware that those from the Bride were hardly audible.

He thought it was shyness.

Now that he had seen her trembling hand, he wondered if perhaps it was fear.

They knelt while they received the Blessing.

Then the Earl was aware, as he had seen it before, that the Marriage Register was waiting for them.

It was not in the Vestry, as was usual, but on a table in front of the empty pews on the left-hand side of the aisle.

Lord Frazer moved towards it, taking his daughter by the arm.

The Earl followed.

The Vicar asked him to sign first, which he did, then handed the quill pen to the Bride.

She had not thrown back her veil as Brides generally did at this moment.

The Earl wondered a little vaguely if he was expected to lift the lace away from her face.

However, he did nothing and she managed to sign her name while still veiled.

Then Lord Frazer said in his usual powerful tone, which seemed to echo round the Church:

"I thought it would be a mistake for there to be any celebrations at the Hall. I have therefore arranged for Ansella's luggage to be taken to the Castle, and it should be there by now. You can go there in the carriage that is waiting for you."

There was nothing the Earl could say, although he thought it strange.

However, it was a relief that he did not have to go to Watton Hall.

He had no wish to watch his Father-in-Law behave as if he had won a major battle.

Which, of course, in actual fact he had!

The carriage was waiting outside the Church, but there was no one to wish the Bride and Bridegroom luck or to throw confetti.

It was a closed carriage, drawn by two horses.

As the Earl got into it, he realised the blinds over the windows were at half-mast.

If he had not been so deeply involved, he would have thought it amusing.

Lord Frazer, having got his own way, and having married his daughter into the British Aristocracy, was now making every effort to prevent anyone knowing how he had achieved it.

They drove back at a very quick pace, the Coachman continually using his whip on the two horses.

The Earl knew, and it was actually a relief, that Lord Frazer would tell no one how he had bought his daughter a title or how much he had paid for it!

As the carriage rocked a little from the pace at which they were travelling through the twisting lanes between the two villages, the Earl asked:

"Are you all right?"

He had not looked at his wife.

Her face was still covered with the veil and she had turned away from him towards the window.

"Yes . . . thank . . . you."

It was a very low, very young voice, and she hesitated before she spoke.

"I can only feel sorry," the Earl went on, "that our first meeting has been such a strange one. I am sure you would have liked to be married with all the usual pomp and ceremony—with Bridesmaids, a huge Reception, and, of course, a very big Wedding-Cake."

He was trying to make himself pleasant.

He was aware that the woman beside him made a little movement, and he had the idea it was a shiver.

Then, as he waited for an answer, she said in a voice he could hardly hear:

"It . . . was . . . what . . . Papa . . . wanted."

There was a twist to the Earl's lips, and he wanted to say he was well aware of that.

Instead, because he thought it was a polite thing to do, he said:

"I am afraid, unless your Father has told you the circumstances in which I find myself, you will find the Castle is not looking as pleasant as it should be."

He had thought when he left the house that morning that it certainly looked much cleaner.

The women had worked very hard the previous day.

There were, however, no flowers in the greenhouses and those in the garden were so overgrown with weeds, they were not worth picking.

His Mother had always had flowers everywhere, especially in the Drawing-Room and her Bedroom.

Also the rooms looked very bare without the ornaments which Basil Burne had removed.

There were spaces on the walls where there had been mirrors which were not in the catalogue.

In the short time he had been home, the Earl had not had a chance of re-arranging the furniture.

Quite a lot appeared to have been moved or disposed of.

So parts of the rooms looked empty, or a piece of furniture which did not fit with the others had been moved in for convenience.

The Bride had made no response to what he had last said.

By now they were nearing his own village.

They passed Monks Wood, then there was the first thatched cottage.

There were very few people about, and the Earl realised they had congregated outside the main gates.

All the village was there.

The Earl had a sudden impulse to bring the carriage to a standstill and introduce his wife to those who had known him all his life.

Then he knew he could not do it.

Suppose she was hideous, or, even worse, for she still had not raised her veil, her face was deformed.

An idea shot through his mind.

Then as they reached the gates a cheer went up.

The Earl lifted the blind on his side of the carriage, pulled down the window, and raised his hand to those who were cheering him.

It took only a few seconds before they were through the gates and into the drive.

Although he had not looked at her, he was aware that his wife had squeezed herself as closely as possible to the side of the carriage.

She obviously wished to avoid being seen.

'She must have something wrong with her,' he thought.

Then it struck him that it was exactly in character for Lord Frazer to wait for an opportunity like this.

So that someone—and it would have to be him—was forced to accept his daughter for what she brought with her.

"I have been caught in a trap," the Earl raged, "and I was a mug not to have realised that was what was happening."

Then he was sensible enough to ask himself what, if he had known, he would have done about it.

The answer was quite clear.

Nothing!

He had to accept the money and the conditions that went with it.

The horses drew up with what was almost a flourish outside the front door.

The whole Staff, including the new members, were waiting to welcome them.

The Earl got out first.

A cheer went up, and one of the younger maids who had only just arrived threw some petals at him.

He was waiting for the Bride to move across the carriage towards the door, but she took a long time about it.

Then, as he put out his hand to help her alight, she stumbled and he knew she was about to fall.

With the deftness and quickness of a man of action, he caught her.

Then, as her head fell against his shoulder, he realised she had fainted.

There was a silence among those who had been waiting to cheer him.

He walked up the steps carrying his Bride, her face still covered by her veil.

She was very light, so light that she seemed little more than a child.

Then, as they reached the Hall, he realised that Mrs. Shepherd, who had come back to him as his Housekeeper, was beside him.

"Take Her Ladyship upstairs, M'Lord," she said, "I'll be as quick as I can, but Ellen'll go with you."

Ellen was one of the young housemaids.

The Earl had seen her working very hard on the Drawing-Room carpet the previous day.

He thought she had appeared to be a sensible young woman.

Now she hurried up the stairs to open the door into the room in which the new Countess was to sleep.

The Earl, against all tradition, had firmly refused to give her his Mother's room.

It had been left exactly as it was before she died.

Even Basil Burne had not altered it.

He had, it was true, sold a number of ornaments and the gold hairbrush set which bore her initials encircled with diamonds.

When Mrs. Shepherd had said that every Countess for several hundred years had slept in that particular room, the Earl had still not relented.

He told them to clean it and then lock the door.

There was another room on the other side of the Master Suite in which he slept.

It was very pleasant and certainly a State Room in the full meaning of the word.

There were no special memories attached to it.

That, he told himself, was quite good enough for Lord Frazer's daughter.

When Ellen opened the door, the Earl saw that Mrs. Shepherd had persuaded the gardeners to find flowers of some description from the garden and round the lake.

They were not all white as they should have been, but at least they were flowers.

They made the room look more attractive than it would have looked otherwise.

Gently the Earl laid his wife down on the bed with its silk and muslin hangings from a golden corolla which touched the ceiling.

She did not move.

Then, steeling himself to know the worst, he picked up her veil and raised it off her face and onto the pillow behind it.

He looked down at his wife with astonishment.

She was not in the least what he expected.

As he had seen in Church, she was very small and very slim.

She might have been younger than the eighteen years he knew her to be.

Her face was heart-shaped.

Her hair was pale gold, like the sun at dawn.

She had a little straight nose and long eyelashes which lay against her pale cheeks.

The Earl drew in his breath.

At least one of his fears was unfounded.

There was nothing ugly or abnormal about his wife.

In fact, she was exceedingly pretty.

Mrs. Shepherd reached his side.

"Now don't you worry, My Lord," she said. "I'll look after Her Ladyship. It's just the excitement of being married, and she'll soon be herself again."

"I am glad you are here, Mrs. Shepherd," the Earl said. "I am sure you will do your best to make her comfortable."

"You knows we'll do that, not only for her but for you, Master Michael," Mrs. Shepherd said. "It's not long since I were sneaking you up a piece of chocolate cake when you'd been sent to bed early for behaving badly."

"Yes, indeed," the Earl said as he smiled, "and that is something I would enjoy now."

"I expect you'll find a surprise when you go downstairs," Mrs. Shepherd said. "Now, you leave the young lady to me and she'll be as right as rain in a short while."

The Earl was only too glad to obey what he thought were very sensible instructions.

He went downstairs to the hall, where the Staff had now gathered from outside.

"Is Her Ladyship all right, M'Lord?" Marlow asked.

"Mrs. Shepherd is looking after her," the Earl answered, "and I am sure she will want to meet you when she feels better."

"I expects it's having th' Wedding in such a hurry that done it," one of the housemaids remarked.

"I am sure that is the truth," the Earl said, "and thank you once again for the good wishes I was not able to hear."

They laughed at that and he walked towards the Drawing-Room.

Marlow followed him.

"I thinks, M'Lord," he said, "that you should have a glass of Champagne on your Wedding Day, if on none other."

"A glass of Champagne?" the Earl asked in surprise.

He had drunk water for dinner the previous night.

He had known without asking that his Uncle would have emptied the cellar.

Marlow gave a chuckle.

"I keeps one bottle hidden away, for when Your Lordship comes back, and believe it or not, I goes and forgets about it until th' Missus reminds me that today be your Wedding Day. Her thinks it's just what you should have with this."

Marlow made a gesture with his hands.

The Earl saw there was a white-iced Wedding-Cake standing on one of the tables.

It was a very small cake.

But the Earl knew they had spent some of the precious money he had given them which had to last until his Wedding.

He was extremely touched.

The cake was made with Mrs. Marlow's usual expertise and ornamented with white flowers on top of it.

"That was very kind of you," he said.

"Us couldn't let you have nothing on your Wedding Day," Marlow said.

He opened the Champagne and the cork came out with a pop.

"Now, that's more like it," he said in a tone of satisfaction.

He poured some of the Champagne into the glass and offered it to the Earl on a small salver.

The Earl took it, and he said:

"I am not drinking alone, Marlow. You must drink with me. You have been here longer than anyone else and it would not seem like home without you."

He saw a suspicion of tears come into the old man's eyes at what he had said.

Marlow turned away to pour himself a small amount of Champagne.

There was a look on his face which told the Earl that whatever happened to him, it would always be a consolation to know that people like Marlow and his wife would love and trust him.

Marlow raised his glass.

"Your health, M'Lord, and may you be happy."

"Thank you," the Earl replied, "and may I say again the Castle would not be home without you and Mrs. Marlow."

The two men drank.

Then, as the Earl put down his glass the door was pushed open.

To his surprise, Ansella came in.

She was still wearing her white gown, but her veil and the wreath had been removed.

As she came towards him he saw that her eyes were very large and seemed to fill her small, pointed face.

"I . . . am . . . sorry," she said breathlessly, "very . . . very . . . sorry . . . but I . . . could . . . not . . . help . . . it."

"Of course not," the Earl said. "And I am sure you should still be resting."

"I . . . thought . . . you would . . . be angry . . . with me," she said, and her voice trembled.

"Marlow, who is our Butler, is just drinking our health," the Earl said, "and now I am going to drink yours."

He poured out half a glass of Champagne and Marlow tactfully moved out of the room.

Then, as the Earl turned round to give it to Ansella, he saw she was looking at the cake.

"Mrs. Marlow, who is the Cook, has made that specially for us," he explained. "It cost money which they should have spent on food for themselves."

As he spoke, he held out the glass of Champagne.

He saw as Ansella took it from him that her hand was trembling as it had in Church.

Then, as she looked up at him, he was aware of the fear in her eyes.

He had never before seen a woman who was so frightened.

Not knowing what to do, the Earl turned round and refilled his own glass.

"Now we must drink to each other," he said. "Although we have had this very strange marriage, I hope in all sincerity I can make you happy."

It was something he would not have been able to say before he had seen her.

She was certainly not the large, overwhelming woman he had expected.

It flashed through his mind that perhaps Lord Frazer had deceived him and she was not his daughter.

She was so different from what he had anticipated and feared.

He could not help wondering if the whole thing was some practical joke on the part of a man who had hated his Father.

While Ansella was signing the Marriage Register, Lord Frazer had put into the Earl's hand a cheque.

He thought at the time it was a rather vulgar and unpleasant way of keeping his word.

But as he put it into the inside pocket of his frock coat, he had just a glimpse of the figures on it and knew he had not been tricked.

"I . . . hope . . . that . . . you . . . will be . . . Happy," Ansella was saying in a shaky voice.

She took a sip of the Champagne, and the Earl said:

"I think you should sit down, and when we have had a slice of Mrs. Marlow's cake so that she will not be disappointed, I am sure you should rest."

She did not reply, and he said:

"You do not have to do anything you do not want to do. But I am sure there will be a special luncheon and if we do not eat it, Mrs. Marlow will be very disappointed.

"I . . . will . . . try," Ansella stammered.

She took another sip of the Champagne as if she felt it fortified her.

The Earl could only look at her in astonishment.

There was no doubt she was very pretty. No, lovely was the right word!

At the same time she was so frightened, he knew that her whole body was trembling beneath the white gown which covered it.

He could never remember a woman being frightened of him before, and he wondered how he could reassure her.

"As you have never been to the Castle," he said, "there are a lot of things I want to show you. But of course you must not get too tired the first day we are married."

Again she did not answer.

He had the feeling she was watching him and shivering even more if he made any movement towards her.

This was something he did not know how to handle. It was with relief that he heard Marlow say:

"Luncheon is served, M'Lady."

Because the words were directed towards her, Ansella turned her head sharply.

Then, as if in some way it had given her a shock, the Champagne glass fell from her hand and smashed on the floor.

# chapter four

"I AM . . . sorry . . . I am . . . sorry," Ansella cried.

"Never mind!" the Earl replied. "I expect we have another glass somewhere."

He tried to pass it off jokingly because he realised how agitated she was.

She went as if to bend down and then stopped suddenly.

"Leave it," the Earl said. "We now have plenty of servants to clear it up."

He went towards the door, and after a moment Ansella followed him.

They walked together down the passage that led to the Dining-Room.

The Earl was wondering what Mrs. Marlow had managed to concoct for them.

He knew the small amount of money he had given them would not have gone far with so many people in the Castle.

There was, however, he discovered, some excellent rabbit soup, which had obviously cost nothing.

A stew followed, but it was difficult to know exactly what was in it.

It was, however, because Mrs. Marlow was a good Cook, very palatable.

The Earl noticed his Bride was still trembling and was eating very little.

In fact, he thought she had hardly eaten enough to feed a mouse.

To relieve the tension, he talked about the trouble on his Estate.

He told her how he had visited the farmers the previous day.

She appeared to be listening, but at the same time he was aware she did not look at him.

In fact, most of the time she looked down and her eyelashes were long against her pale cheeks.

When the stew was finished, Marlow brought in the Wedding-Cake, which they had not touched.

He put it down in front of the Earl.

It was a very small cake, and he said:

"I suppose really I should cut it with my sword, but I think if I did so, it might disintegrate altogether."

Marlow gave him a knife and he cut two slices of the cake and one was served to Ansella.

They drank during the meal what was left of the bottle of Champagne, or at least the Earl did.

Ansella just sipped from her glass.

The Earl thought perhaps it was because she was afraid of dropping another one.

He knew of course it would be a mistake to make any comment.

The meal was just finished when Marlow came in to say there was someone from the Solicitors in Oxford.

The Earl looked up eagerly.

He had been expecting this and had made his arrangements the previous day.

He had sent Wicks into Oxford with a letter to his
Solicitors to tell them what he required.

He told them frankly that he was being lent twenty-
five thousand pounds by Lord Frazer.

They would receive the cheque as soon as the Marriage had taken place.

What he asked them to do was to persuade the Bank
where his Father had dealt for so long to advance him
two thousand pounds.

The cheque would be in their hands as soon as possible.

He then required the Solicitors to send one of their
most efficient Accountants to distribute the money in the
village.

It would naturally be more convenient if it was already packaged before he came with it.

The Earl told the Solicitors his Staff were to have the
same wages as they had before he went to India.

Also they would receive three months back payment
as well as wages in advance for the next three weeks.

He felt sure he had thought of everything.

Now he said to Ansella:

"I will tell you what is happening after I have seen
this man. I am afraid it will take a little time, so go into
the Drawing-Room and I will join you there as soon as
I can."

She did not answer him but walked obediently towards the door.

He held it open for her.

As she passed, her arm brushed lightly against him,
and he was aware that she started and moved quickly
forward.

For the first time he wondered if what she felt for him
was not only fear but repulsion.

It was, however, at this moment more important to talk to the Accountant than to worry about anything else.

He opened the Drawing-Room door for Ansella, then hurried to his Father's Study.

The man who was waiting for him was middle-aged and had been with the Solicitors for many years.

He knew everything about the Estate and the terrible condition in which the Earl had found it on his return.

"I think, My Lord," he said politely, "you are being extremely generous to your people and I am sure they will appreciate it."

"They have been on the verge of starvation for nearly a month," the Earl answered, "and it is something your firm should have discovered and done something about."

"I am sure, My Lord, we would have done so had we realised that Mr. Burne was leaving the country," the Accountant replied. "But he had been exceedingly rude to everyone who approached him after you left, and told them to 'mind their own business.' "

The Earl realised that in those circumstances there was nothing the Solicitors could have done since he had given his Uncle Power of Attorney.

"Never, never for the rest of my life," he vowed to himself, "will I ever delegate authority again."

The Accountant, whose name was Weaver, opened a leather case and showed him the money neatly packed as he had suggested.

"Your Lordship did not state how many people there were."

"I am not sure myself," the Earl replied. "We know, of course, how many were employed before my Father died, but while I have been away some of the young men have left to find employment elsewhere and I think the same applies to the women."

"I shall soon find out," Mr. Weaver said. "Your Lordship's Head Groom informed me that as there seemed no premises large enough in the village to hold everyone who would be waiting, they have opened the Church."

The Earl laughed.

"I certainly did not think of that," he said, "but it is a very sensible solution, and it means those who have to wait for some time can at least sit down."

Mr. Weaver smiled.

"That is what I thought, My Lord, and they are certainly all receiving a blessing."

"And not before it was time," the Earl retorted.

He handed Mr. Weaver the cheque that he had received from Lord Frazer.

He thought that the Accountant took it with an expression of relief on his face.

After all the preparations they had made, it would have been very embarrassing if at the last moment Lord Frazer had gone back on his word.

But he had kept it!

The Earl looked down with satisfaction at the sum that was written in his large, untidy hand-writing.

Mr. Weaver put it away very carefully in the pocket of his coat.

He handed the Earl some packages from his case, then closed it.

"Now, My Lord," he said, "I think I should be getting down to business. I saw quite a crowd waiting for me when I passed the Church just now."

The Earl escorted him to the front door.

He waited while he stepped into the carriage which had fetched him from Oxford.

It was then he remembered he had told his wife to wait for him in the Drawing-Room.

For a moment he contemplated doing something else first.

Then he told himself he must behave properly on his Wedding Day.

He had no wish for Ansella to be able to complain that he had neglected her.

There were two footmen on duty in the hall.

When he was aware they were Colin and his friend, he stopped to ask them how they were getting on.

"Fine, M'Lord, just fine," Colin replied, "and me Father asked me to tell yer they had a real feast yesterday with the money yer gives 'em. There wasn't a soul in the village who didn't thank Yer Lordship for every mouthful."

"I am glad to hear that," the Earl replied. "Now you two must help Marlow as much as you can. He has had a very hard time recently and he is not as young as he used to be."

"Us be doing everythin' he tells us," Colin assured the Earl.

"That is what I like to hear," he said.

As he spoke, Marlow came hurrying into the hall.

"I'm sorry, M'Lord," he apologised, "I didn't know the gentleman was leaving."

"It is all right," the Earl replied, "and give this to Mrs. Marlow and tell her to buy everything we require."

He put into Marlow's hands a small bag the Accountant had given him.

It contained fifty pounds and he had another fifty pounds for himself.

Marlow took the bag and stared at it.

"For the moment," the Earl said quietly, "we must pay the shop in the village, and anything we buy from the farms, in cash."

Marlow understood.

"We'll do that, M'Lord."

His voice and the expression on his face told the Earl how much this meant.

"And this is for you and your wife," the Earl said, giving him another bag.

It contained, as Marlow knew, his wages.

He looked so emotional that the Earl said hurriedly: "You deserve that and much more!"

He walked towards the Drawing-Room.

When he opened the door he thought at first there was no one in the room.

Ansella must have gone upstairs or into the garden.

Then he saw that she was lying curled up on the sofa.

Her head was on a satin cushion and she was fast asleep.

He thought, considering how frightened she had been at the Marriage Service, and how little she had eaten at luncheon, that she was exhausted.

Perhaps it was because, like himself, she had not slept last night.

He moved quietly towards the fireplace, on one side of which was the sofa.

Then, as he stood looking at her, he was aware there was something on her white gown.

She had fallen asleep facing the back of the sofa.

The Earl thought at first it was a flower which had somehow become attached to the white silk of which her gown was made.

Then he was aware there was also something red on the base of her neck.

Because he was curious, he moved a little closer to the sofa.

He saw that the white gown she had worn for her Wedding had obviously been intended as a simple evening-gown for unimportant occasions.

He had noticed at luncheon that it was cut fairly low in the front.

Round her neck was a necklace of three strings of pearls which covered much of her skin.

At the back there was nothing below the clasp of the necklace.

As he reached the sofa he realised what he had been seeing was not, as he had thought, the petals of a flower, but blood.

'She must have scratched herself,' he supposed, and wondered how she had done it.

There was also blood coming through the back of her gown lower down.

Automatically he drew out his handkerchief.

Then, as he knelt down to wipe away the blood from her skin, hoping he would not wake her, he saw there were marks on either side of the blood.

Incredible though it seemed, they appeared to be the weals caused by a whip.

Very gently he wiped away the large drop of blood.

As he did so, Ansella opened her eyes, then gave a little scream.

"Do not be frightened," the Earl said, "but there is blood on your neck and I am trying to wipe it away."

"It . . . hurts . . . it hurts . . . terribly," she murmured.

"What happened to you?" the Earl asked. "Did you have a fall?"

He was sure it was something quite different but did not like to say so.

Ansella did not answer and winced at the touch of his handkerchief.

"You are bleeding," he said very quietly, "a little lower down your back also. It is going to spoil your dress, and I think perhaps you should have it properly seen to."

Ansella made a hasty movement and sat up.

He realised it hurt her to do so and she stifled a cry.

The Earl sat down at the side of the sofa.

"What has happened?" he asked. "I cannot imagine how you could have hurt your back in such a nasty manner."

She looked at him with large, frightened eyes, and her lips quivered.

"Tell me what happened," the Earl said coaxingly. "It would be a great mistake for us to start our married life by having secrets from each other."

"You will . . . not tell . . . Papa I . . . told . . . you?"

The words were almost inaudible, but the Earl heard them and shook his head.

"I will not tell your Father or anyone else what you tell me," he said. "But I want to help you and to stop you from feeling any more pain."

"It . . . hurts and . . . hurts," Ansella murmured. "I could . . . not sleep . . . last night but I did . . . not dare ask . . . anyone to . . . put anything . . . on . . . it."

It was quite a long sentence, and she said it hesitatingly.

Watching her, the Earl knew she was afraid of his reaction.

"Of course you should have had it seen to," he answered. "But you have not told me what happened."

She turned her head away so that he could see only her profile.

Then she said in a whisper.

"Papa . . . beat . . . me."

It was what the Earl had suspected.

Even so, he found it hard to credit that any man would beat anything so small and frightened.

"Why did he whip you?" he asked.

There was a pause, then Ansella said:

"If I . . . tell you . . . then you . . . too will . . . be angry."

"I promise not to be angry," the Earl replied. "But I suspect, although I may be wrong, that you were refusing to marry me."

"I . . . ran . . . away," Ansella said. "I did . . . not get . . . very far and . . . Papa was . . . very . . . very . . . angry."

"So he whipped you," the Earl murmured.

He thought it was just the sort of bestial cruelty he would expect from Lord Frazer.

Then he realised that Ansella was looking at him as if she expected him to be as angry as her Father had been.

"I can understand what you felt," he said, "because I wanted to run away myself."

"You ... did not ... want to ... marry ... me?"

"I did not want to marry anyone," the Earl answered, "especially someone I had never seen and who had never seen me."

She gave a deep sigh almost as if it were a relief to know that he could have felt like that.

Then she said:

"If you ... did not ... want to ... marry me ... how did ... Papa make ... you?"

The Earl was surprised.

He had thought that Lord Frazer would certainly have told his daughter what the marriage was costing him.

After a moment he said:

"I see I must tell you the whole story and how very grateful I am for your help. At the same time, it was very hard for both of us."

Still, she did not say anything.

She was just sitting looking at him with her frightened eyes.

"I have a long story to tell you," the Earl said. "But I think first we should do something to stop your back from hurting you."

"No! No!" Ansella cried quickly. "I do not ... want anyone to ... see it. They might ... tell Papa or ... somehow he ... would hear ... about it and ... then he ... would ... whip me ... again."

"That is something he will never do again," the Earl replied firmly. "You are now my wife, and as my wife no other man, and that includes your Father, will ever touch you."

Ansella's eyes seemed to grow even wider than they were already.

"Do . . . do you . . . really . . . mean . . . that?" she asked.

"I mean it," the Earl said, "and you can trust me to protect you from your Father and anyone else assaulting you in any way."

He could not help his voice sharpening as he mentioned her Father.

Then he added:

"Has he often beaten you in this appalling manner?"

"Mama . . . would not . . . let him . . . when she . . . was . . . alive," Ansella replied, "but then . . . he beat my . . . horse or . . . my dog, and if he . . . hears that . . . I have told . . . you or . . . anyone else . . . if he cannot . . . beat me he . . . will beat . . . them."

The Earl could hardly believe what he was hearing.

He felt his anger rise within him at the thought of any man behaving so cruelly.

Without saying anything, he rose and jerked at the bell-pull at the side of the fireplace.

"What is your horse's name?" he asked Ansella.

She was staring at him because she was not certain what he was doing, or why

She did not answer him immediately.

Then she said:

"It is . . . *Firefly*, but . . . why do . . . you want . . . to know?"

"And your dog?"

"*Rufus*," she answered.

The door opened as she spoke, and Marlow came in.

"Send a vehicle of some sort to Watton Hall," the Earl said, "to collect Her Ladyship's dog *Rufus*, and a groom is to travel with it to bring back her horse *Firefly*."

"Very good, M'Lord," Marlow replied. "But I be wondering what we could send. Wicks and the carriage be awaiting to take th' gentleman back to Oxford."

"I know that," the Earl replied. "But I think for some reason of his own, Wicks was driving only one horse."

He paused a moment and then went on:

"There is another in the Stable, and the old brake, in which I remember you and other members of the Staff travelled when my Father went to London, is still there."

"So it is, M'Lord," Marlow said with a smile. "I'd almost forgotten them days."

"Well, tell one of the new men working in the Stables to leave at once," the Earl said. "There is no need to ask permission of Lord Frazer, just collect the horse and the dog."

Marlow went from the room and Ansella said:

"Thank you ... thank ... you. I never ... thought you ... would want ... my horse in ... your Stables or ... my dog in ... your ... Castle."

"There have always been dogs in the Castle," the Earl answered. "But I have learnt my Uncle disposed of them after I left for India."

He spoke bitterly and Ansella said:

"That ... must have ... hurt you ... as it hurt ... me when Papa beat ... *Rufus* and he ... did not ... understand."

There was a break in her voice and the Earl had an impulse to put his arm around her as if she were a child and tell her such a thing would never happen again.

Instead, he said:

"Now, what I am going to do is to get some Healing Cream which my Mother used to make for anyone in the village who cut or bruised themselves. I am sure there will be some left and I will ask my housekeeper, Mrs. Shepherd, to find me a pot."

"You will ... not tell ... her what ... it is ... for?" Ansella said quickly.

"Not if you do not want me to," the Earl said.

"She might ... somehow talk ... and if she ... did and ... Papa knew—"

She stopped, and the Earl thought she was shivering.

"I think your Father would find it very difficult to hear what goes on in my Castle," he said. "As I expect you know, my Father and your Father never spoke to each other except to quarrel."

Ansella nodded, which told him she did know, and he continued:

"The servants who have been here for years and those who live in the village have always taken our side in the dispute over Monks Wood. Now you belong to us, but the animosity towards your Father will continue."

As he finished speaking, he went towards the door.

He told Colin, who was in the hall, to find Mrs. Shepherd.

He was to ask her for a pot of Healing Cream which he was certain was somewhere in the housekeeper's room.

Colin hurried up the stairs to obey, and the Earl went back to the Drawing-Room.

He saw as he entered that Ansella was holding his blood-stained handkerchief in her hand and looking at it ruefully.

As he joined her she said:

"Will not . . . your Valet . . . think that . . . this looks . . . very strange?"

"I shall tell him I had a nose-bleed," the Earl replied.

For the first time, there was just a faint smile on Ansella's lips.

Then she gave a little chuckle.

"Do you think . . . he will believe . . . you?" she asked.

"Of course he will," the Earl replied. "I think very positively, I speak very positively, and I do not expect anyone to question the truth of what I say."

Again there was a faint smile on her lips before she said:

"One can . . . never be . . . quite certain . . . of that."

"Anyway, he would be too polite to question whether it is the truth or not," the Earl replied.

He sat down on the sofa as he had before.

To make room for him, Ansella pulled her legs a little closer.

As she did so, he realised she winced.

"I will do what I can to help make your back feel better," he said. "But if it is still very bad tomorrow, I think you will have to see a Doctor."

"The Doctor will not ... come to the Hall," Ansella replied, "because Papa was ... so rude to him when ... Mama died and ... said it was ... all his ... fault."

It was the sort of thing, the Earl thought, that he would expect Lord Frazer to say.

"There are plenty of good Doctors in Oxford," he said, "and we will have the best."

As he spoke, he realised that a Doctor from Oxford would be expensive.

He would be spending the money that he needed on the land and for his own people.

At the same time, Ansella was entitled to it, although apparently, which seemed extraordinary, she had no idea why their marriage had taken place in such a strange manner.

The Earl waited until Marlow appeared with a pot of his Mother's Healing Cream on a silver salver.

"Mrs. Shepherd has asked me to tell you, M'Lord," Marlow said, "that there be only three pots left. As she often made the cream with Her Ladyship, she thinks perhaps you'd wish her to make some more in case it was wanted in the village."

"An excellent idea," the Earl answered. "Tell her to make some as soon as she has time to find the herbs my Mother always used. I suppose they are still growing in the garden."

"They be in the Herb Garden right enough, M'Lord," Marlow said. "I understands Mr. Cosnat'll be working in it as soon as he's cleared the garden Your Lordship sees from the windows."

"Good," the Earl approved. "Then Her Ladyship will have the flowers which I am sure she will want in every room just as it used to be."

Marlow smiled and went from the room.

As the door shut, Ansella said:

"How . . . did . . . you know . . . I love . . . flowers?"

"Of course you love flowers, every woman wants flowers around her. And flowers given as a compliment to her tell her how beautiful she is."

The Earl was speaking as he might have spoken to one of the women who had charmed him in Simla.

As he finished speaking he saw Ansella was looking at him in surprise.

It was as if she had never imagined he would say anything like that.

"Now, this cream," he began, "is magical. Every time my Mother used it on children or grown-ups, they said she had waved a magic wand, and what they were suffering from had healed overnight."

"I hope . . . you are . . . right," Ansella said. "My back . . . hurt so much last night . . . that I . . . wished I could . . . die."

"I promise you it is not going to hurt tonight," the Earl said.

As he spoke the last words, he saw by the expression on her face that the idea of tonight was something which was frightening her.

Then he knew instinctively why she had run away.

It was not only because she did not wish to marry a man she had never seen, but also because she was afraid of all men.

It was understandable, considering she had lived with a brute like her Father.

She was expecting her husband to be as cruel or perhaps even crueller.

Very quickly the Earl said:

"Now, suppose you turn round. I promise you I will be very gentle and try not to hurt you."

Obediently, like a small child, Ansella did as she was told.

The Earl first wiped away the blood which was showing again at the base of her neck.

The red patch on her gown a little lower down was larger than it had been when he had first seen it.

"Would you mind very much," he asked, "if I unbuttoned your gown? There is a place which is bleeding about four inches down your back and apart from hurting you it is certainly ruining your dress."

"That . . . means the . . . maids will . . . see it," Ansella whispered.

The Earl knew that once again she was thinking of what would happen if this was reported to her Father.

"I am going to make sure," he said, "that the only person who sees your back and attends to your dress is Mrs. Shepherd."

He paused a moment and then went on very softly:

"She has been here at the Castle since I was born, which is twenty-seven years ago, and she thinks of herself as one of our family. Our loves are her loves and our hates are her hates."

"What . . . you are . . . saying," Ansella said slowly, "is . . . that because your Father . . . hated Papa . . . she . . . hates him . . . too."

"Exactly," the Earl agreed. "So he will never know what has happened here today or any day so long as you are my wife."

He thought that Ansella gave a little sigh of relief.

Very gently he undid the four top buttons of her gown.

The sight of the weals from the whip Lord Frazer had used on her appalled him.

One, as he had already discovered, was bleeding badly.

He stanched Ansella's wounds with the Healing Cream, and although she winced several times, she did not make a sound.

There were, the Earl thought, more marks further down but the majority were on her shoulders and the top of her back.

He guessed, although he did not like to ask questions, that when she had run away, Lord Frazer had followed her on horseback.

He had whipped her while she was standing up.

That would certainly account for where the marks were situated.

The whip Lord Frazer had used was obviously one of the tips used by jockeys, and by some breeders on their dogs.

Ansella's skin was very white and soft.

It was difficult for the Earl to credit that any man could be so brutal.

When he had covered every weal he could see with the cream, he did up the buttons at the back of her dress.

"Now, you are not to worry," he said. "As I have told you, only Mrs. Shepherd will know what has happened and I want you to allow her to apply some more cream to your back before you go to bed. I think, unless you want to make a mess of the sheets, you had better let her put something protective over it."

"Yes . . . yes . . . of course," Ansella agreed, "and . . . thank you for . . . being so . . . kind."

"I am just horrified that this should have happened to you on my account," the Earl said.

"I did . . . not expect . . . you to be . . . kind," Ansella said.

"Had you not heard of me before you were told to marry me?" the Earl asked.

"I knew that you lived at the Castle and that when your Father ... died you ... became the ... Earl. But I had never ... seen you ... and Papa was so ... angry over Monks Wood that he never ... talked about ... you or your ... family."

The Earl thought that was actually a relief, but he said:

"It must have been a shock to be told that you were to marry one of your Father's enemies."

"I thought it ... was very ... strange," Ansella said. "But I ... did not ... want to marry ... anyone unless I ... fell in love."

"That is exactly how I felt too," the Earl remarked.

"Then why did ... you let Papa ... make us ... marry each ... other?" Ansella questioned.

"I will tell you the whole story," the Earl said, "and then I think you will understand."

He told her how excited he had been when he was asked to go out to India.

He wanted to be with a man he had always admired and with whom he had hunted in Ireland.

She listened to everything he said like a child hearing a fairy story.

Her eyes were fixed on his as if she were frightened of missing anything.

It mirrored the different emotions he aroused by what he was telling her.

He knew she was fascinated as he explained how he had ridden with the Viceroy to the famine areas, how they had attended the Durbar of Princes and stayed in fantastic Palaces in their journeys round India.

Then he related how the Viceroy was murdered by a Pathan.

There had been no special reason for it except that the man had a grudge against the world because he was in prison.

Ansella's eyes clouded.

Because it was such a tragic story, the Earl's voice, without his realising it, was very moving.

When he finished describing how the Viceroy had died in the launch going back to the ship, his voice broke.

Then there were tears in Ansella's eyes.

"How ... could it have ... happened to such a ... wonderful man?" she asked.

"That is what I wanted to know," the Earl replied. "India was not India without him, so I came home as quickly as I could."

He then went on to tell her what he had discovered— the condition of the Castle, the land uncultivated, and the people in the village starving.

"I had ... no idea of this," Ansella exclaimed. "How ... could that ... happen so near ... to us and Papa never ... speak of ... it?"

The Earl wanted to say that he thought Lord Frazer might have given a helping hand to the people who were suffering so near to him.

He just went on to tell how he had visited his Solicitors in Oxford.

He had found everything he possessed in the way of stocks and shares had been sold and the money in the Bank withdrawn.

"So ... you have ... literally nothing?" Ansella asked.

"Just what I had in my pocket which was left over from my journey," the Earl replied. "As I have already told you, my Uncle sold everything that was available in the Castle."

"He was ... wicked ... a very ... wicked man," Ansella cried.

"But the wicked 'flourish like a green bay tree,' " the Earl quoted, "and that is what he is undoubtedly doing at the moment in America."

"I cannot ... believe that he will ... not be ... punished in some ... way or ... another," Ansella said.

85

There was a silence, and then the Earl said:

"Now, this is where you came into the picture."

She looked at him enquiringly.

He told her how he was on his way back from Oxford when he called at Watton Hall.

"Your Father was the only person I could think of at the moment to whom I had anything to offer," he said, "and that, of course, was Monks Wood."

"Papa had ... always believed ... it to be ... his," Ansella said.

"Just as my Father was convinced that from the beginning of time it was ours," the Earl replied.

"And ... when ... you offered it ... to Papa ... what did ... he say?"

The Earl hesitated for a moment, then he told the truth.

"He said he would lend me all the money I needed to save my people from starvation, but I had to marry his daughter."

"Why should ... he say ... that," Ansella asked, "when he has always ... hated your ... Father?"

Again the Earl paused, then he thought it best for her to know the truth from the very beginning.

"Your Father is socially ambitious," he said, "and the Earls of Rayburne are the head of one of the oldest families in England."

He continued with pride in his voice:

"They have been Statesmen, soldiers, and sailors and all have distinguished themselves. They have all looked on the Castle as home. Each Earl of Rayburne who lives in it is the head of the family."

"So that is ... what Papa ... wanted for ... me?" Ansella said.

"Exactly," the Earl agreed, "but he does not want the world to know that he forced us both to be married before we had even met."

"Then . . . why did . . . you not make . . . him wait?" Ansella enquired.

"Because, as I have already explained, my people were starving and your Father would not give me the cheque until you signed the Marriage Register in the Church."

Ansella obviously thought this very strange. But she said aloud:

"He did say the other morning . . . almost as if he was talking . . . to himself, that he would put . . . our Marriage in the *Gazette* in . . . a fortnight's time . . . but I did not . . . know what . . . he meant."

"What he meant," the Earl said, "was that people should think that when I came back from India I had had time to renew the friendship which we presumably had, being neighbours, before I left, and that our marriage did not take place on the spur of the moment without any normal reason for it."

He spoke somewhat bitterly, and Ansella murmured:

"I am sorry . . . I am . . . sorry . . . of course you . . . must feel . . . like this and it was . . . very wrong of Papa . . . not to have given . . . you time . . ."

Her voice died away, and she said:

"I expect he thought that if . . . you met me . . . you would think I was . . . a bore which he . . . always says . . . I am and . . . very stupid. So you would . . . not have . . . wanted to . . . marry me."

She was thinking it out for herself and the Earl thought very intelligently.

"I am sure," he said, "your Father does not really think of you like that."

"But he . . . does," Ansella insisted. "He really . . . hates me because I am . . . not a boy. My Mama told me . . . how when I was . . . born he was . . . angry with her because he was . . . certain I would be . . . a son."

The Earl thought the more he heard about Lord Frazer, the more he despised him.

He then could not refrain from asking:

"Why did your Mother marry your Father?"

"I think it was ... really because he was ... very rich and Mama's parents were ... very poor. But she also thought in ... those days when he was ... young that he was ... very smart and dashing. She had not met ... many men and it was very ... exciting to have a man ... like Papa ... begging her to be ... his wife."

"Then who are your Mother's parents?" the Earl asked.

"Mama's Father was Sir Walter Lansdale, and although his family is not as old as yours, Grandpapa was the Fifth Baronet."

Now the Earl understood.

Lord Frazer had not only bought his daughter into the Social World, but he had also bought his wife.

His money had come from shipping in Liverpool.

As an ambitious man, he had always been aware that the Frazers were of no social importance.

Their blood was certainly not blue.

"Was your Mother happy?" the Earl asked quietly.

"I think she was very happy when they were first married," Ansella answered. "But as he got older Papa grew more and more difficult, especially when the Doctor said she could have ... no more ... children."

The Earl was aware that this must have been a bitter blow.

"He was kind to me at times, especially when Mama was alive," Ansella went on. "But after she died I always seemed to be doing ... something ... wrong."

There was no need to ask what happened when she did, and the Earl said quickly:

"That is all over now. You are going to lead an entirely new life and the first thing I am going to do is to ask you for your help."

"My help?" Ansella asked in astonishment.

"It is going to be quite a heavy task," the Earl said with a smile. "Therefore you have got to hurry up and heal your back as quickly as you can. But that means you must rest it."

She looked at him enquiringly and he knew that at the back of her mind she was still very frightened of him.

"I think, Ansella," he said, "the first thing we both have to do is to get to know each other. So let us pretend we have just met for the first time. You have been introduced to me as the Honourable Ansella Frazer and I as the Earl of Rayburne."

As he spoke, the Earl put out his hand:

"How do you do?" he said. "It is very nice to meet you."

Ansella gave a little chuckle.

"That seems . . . very strange," she said.

"Not at all," the Earl answered, "and I would like you to say that you are pleased to meet me."

"But . . . I am," she said. "I . . . really . . . am."

As she spoke she took her hand away from his, and he was aware she was trembling.

There was also undoubtedly the same touch of fear in her eyes.

# chapter five

"Now, what would you like to do?" the Earl asked.

He looked out of the window as he spoke and saw that the sun was shining.

He thought if he had a choice, the one thing he would like to do was to go riding.

However, that was not possible at the moment, and he wondered how he could entertain his wife.

"What . . . I would . . . like if it . . . would not . . . bore you," Ansella said nervously, "is to see your . . . Library if . . . you have one."

"Of course I have one," the Earl replied, "and I shall be delighted to show it to you."

She rose almost eagerly from the sofa.

He thought it was a strange request.

Most women he knew were not interested in books, especially if they could talk to him instead.

However, he led her down the long corridor which led to the Library and opened the door.

To his relief, his Uncle had not altered the Library in any way.

He suspected that some of the valuable books had disappeared, but certainly the great majority were there.

The Library had been beautifully planned.

The bookcases covered the walls and jutted out into the room.

Along one side a balcony gave access to the upper shelves which was reached by a spiral staircase. He remembered climbing up it as a boy.

He walked to the fireplace from which was the best view of the whole room.

It had tall Georgian windows reaching almost to the ceiling.

The curtains which covered them were a deep crimson velvet.

"There are about two thousand books here," he said.

"I . . . want to . . . read them . . . all," Ansella replied in a rapt little voice.

The Earl laughed.

"That will take you some time."

"I have never . . . seen such a . . . wonderful collection," she went on. "Papa has . . . quite a . . . good Library but . . . nothing like . . . this."

"I do not need to ask you," he said, "if you enjoy reading."

"I read and read . . . whenever I . . . get the . . . chance," Ansella replied.

"Why?" the Earl asked.

It was a question he would have not asked another woman.

He knew the women with whom he had flirted in India read novels only if they were popular.

They were much more interested in live men like himself than in the heroes they read about in books.

"It is . . . the only . . . way I can . . . travel," Ansella said. "I can . . . see the . . . places I read . . . about in my . . . imagination, but I would . . . really like to . . . see them with . . . my own eyes."

"One day I must take you to India," the Earl said. "It is so beautiful and I know you will be thrilled by the Taj Mahal and the other buildings like it."

"I have read . . . about it and it . . . would be the . . . most wonderful thing . . . that could . . . happen to . . . me," Ansella said.

"I wonder why your Father did not take you travelling," the Earl said.

"Before I grew up," Ansella answered, "I was too busy with my teachers and tutors . . . to leave home."

The Earl raised his eyebrows.

"Teachers and tutors?" he repeated.

There was a little pause, and then Ansella said:

"Because Papa was . . . so angry I was . . . not a boy, he gave me what he . . . thought was . . . a boy's education. I learnt Latin, Greek, French, and all the other subjects which I expect you . . . learnt at . . . school."

The Earl was astonished.

At the same time, he knew Lord Frazer was punishing his daughter for being the wrong sex.

"As you are so good at languages," he said, "when I can afford it, which I am afraid will not be for a long time, I must certainly take you abroad."

Ansella clasped her hands together.

"That is the most . . . exciting thing I have . . . ever heard. But I am so . . . afraid it will not . . . happen."

"It will happen," the Earl said firmly. "In the meantime you will have to be content with my books."

"I have told . . . you already I intend to . . . read every one of . . . them," Ansella answered.

He laughed.

Then, to please her, he picked out some of the books he remembered which were particularly rare.

A first edition of Shakespeare's *Midsummer Night's Dream* was one, another was by Chaucer.

He liked the way that Ansella handled them.

It was almost reverently and so very carefully that she turned over the leaves.

He was then aware when he looked out of the window that the sun was still shining.

He wanted to be in the fresh air.

"If it is not too tiring," he said, "I would like to show you what I think is the most beautiful view in the world."

"I would . . . love to see . . . that," Ansella answered.

"I am afraid it means climbing up some very steep steps," he said. "Are you sure you are not too tired?"

"My back is so much . . . better since you put . . . the cream on it," she said. "It is hardly . . . hurting at . . . all."

"Very well," the Earl said, "we will go up to the Tower, but you must promise that if you feel too tired to do any more, you must tell me so."

"I promise," Ansella said solemnly.

He put back the books they had been looking at.

As they moved away from the shelves, the Earl saw that Ansella touched them very gently, as she might caress a dog or a child.

It made him realise she was not pretending when she said she wanted to read everything in the Library.

It made her very different from the other women he had known.

They went further down the passage until they reached the door to the Tower.

"This is the oldest part of the Castle," the Earl explained. "The Tower dates back to Norman times, and I must find the history of it for you."

"I would like that," Ansella said.

He opened the Tower door.

There was the Guard Room and the narrow stone steps spiralling up past the arrow-slit windows.

The Earl went up first, slowly, so that Ansella would not tire herself by hurrying.

When he reached the top, he opened the door onto the roof and stepped out into the sunshine.

He went to the side of the battlement.

As Ansella joined him he gestured with his hand towards the magnificent view stretching to the hazy horizon.

Then he waited to see what she would say.

She stood in silence for quite a long time before she said:

"It is lovely, very, very beautiful, more beautiful than anything I have ever seen."

"That is what I feel every time I come here," the Earl said. "It is a great satisfaction to know that many acres of it belong to me."

"It must make you very proud," Ansella said, "but I understand it is also a . . . great . . . responsibility."

He knew as she spoke she was thinking of the money he had had to obtain from her Father because he needed it for what he called "his people."

Because he did not want to dwell on money at the moment, he said:

"It is from here on top of the Tower that those guarding it could watch any approaching enemy. They could hardly be attacked without prior warning of it."

"I can see that," Ansella said, "and they shot at them with their bows and arrows."

"The history books tell us they defended it very successfully," the Earl said.

Ansella was looking down over the edge of the Tower and gave an exclamation.

"You have a moat!" she said. "I have read about moats but I have never seen one."

"I am afraid this is a poor example," the Earl replied, "because when later they repaired and built additions to the Castle they drained away most of the moat because it was soaking into the stonework and making the walls insecure."

"There is some water left," Ansella said, looking at the deep pool just below.

"Yes, that is still there," the Earl said. "It used to fascinate me when I was a little boy because those guarding the Castle when they took prisoners would usually end up throwing them heavily bound into the moat so that they were drowned."

Ansella did not speak, and he added quickly:

"It was very cruel and something we do not want to remember today."

"I am not ... sure," Ansella said slowly, "if it is not ... kinder for ... someone to ... die than to be ... a prisoner."

"Why do you say that?" the Earl asked.

"I often think," she said, "of the poor Frenchman who built the wonderful *Château* of the Vaux-le-Vicomte in the Seventeenth Century."

"I remember reading about it," the Earl said, "but I have not seen it."

"It was so beautiful and so grand," Ansella went on, "that Louis XIV, the Sun King, was jealous because he thought it was finer than Versailles. So he put the poor man who had built it in prison for nineteen years and he never saw his beautiful *Château* again."

"I remember the story now," the Earl said, "and I thought it was a hard punishment for trying to be too grand."

"I am sure he would rather have died," Ansella said, "than sit day after day thinking of his lovely *Château* which he could not see."

The Earl realised the story had moved her, and he said:

"I think most of the prisoners are always hopeful they will sooner or later be released."

"The Russians tortured their prisoners," Ansella said. "Even Peter the Great was incredibly cruel to his son, and although he did not actually murder him, he had him . . . tortured and . . . beaten . . . until . . . he died."

Now there was a note in her voice which told the Earl those things really upset her.

'She is certainly original!' he thought. 'Very different from any other woman I have ever met.'

Thinking that the conversation was somewhat morbid, he looked in the other direction.

He saw the old brake coming up the drive.

"You are just about to have a visitor," he said aloud, "and you should go down to welcome him."

Ansella looked at him questioningly.

Then, turning to the direction in which he had been looking, she gave an exclamation.

"It is *Rufus*!" she cried. "Oh, are you quite certain they will have collected him?"

She did not wait for the Earl's answer.

She ran to the door at the top of the Tower and began to go down the spiral steps.

The Earl folowed her.

He was not surprised when she reached the ground floor that without waiting for him she ran down the long corridor which led to the hall.

As she got there, the brake had drawn up outside the front door.

One of the footmen had just let out a small red-coated Spaniel.

When the dog saw Ansella at the top of the steps, he gave a bark of excitement and ran up them.

By the time the Earl joined his wife, *Rufus* was jumping up at her and barking with excitement.

He thought as she knelt down to hug him that they made a very pretty picture.

"*Rufus*! *Rufus*!" Ansella was saying. "Are you all right? I am sure you missed me and now you have found me again."

There was no doubt about *Rufus*'s excitement, and the Earl went through the open door.

As he stood on the steps he saw, as he expected, a horse coming up the drive.

It was being ridden very carefully by one of his newly engaged grooms.

He turned back with a smile to say to Ansella:

"You have another visitor who I am sure will be just as pleased to see you as *Rufus*."

Ansella jumped up and joined the Earl.

"It is *Firefly*!" she said. "Oh, how can I ever thank you!"

She did not wait for his reply but ran down the steps and across the Courtyard towards her horse.

It was a very fine looking animal, and the Earl thought that he could not criticise Lord Frazer when it came to horse-flesh.

Ansella was hugging and patting *Firefly*, who was nuzzling against her.

The Earl joined them and thanked the groom for having collected him.

"Was there any difficulty?" he asked in a low voice.

"No, M'Lord," the groom replied. "In fact, they says as how they didn't think 'Er Ladyship'd manage without 'er horse and 'er dog. So they weren't surprised when us arrived."

Looking at his wife, the Earl realised she looked a completely different woman.

Her eyes were shining and she was smiling as she talked and patted both *Firefly* and *Rufus*.

He could understand they were the only two creatures she had to love.

After her Mother died, she had been left alone with her Father.

He hoped now that her horse and her dog were at the Castle they would help her get over her fear of him.

He could not understand why she was so frightened.

Sooner or later he would have to find out the real reason for it.

'It is that ghastly Father of hers,' he thought, and found it difficult to believe that any man could behave as Lord Frazer had done.

Because he thought Ansella would be over-tired, he insisted that *Firefly* be taken to the Stables.

She very reluctantly let *Firefly* go, and the Earl said:

"When he has settled down in what I promise you will be a comfortable stall, you will be able to go and say good night to him."

"I want to do that because it is something I have always done," Ansella replied. "Sometimes, when Papa said it was a lot of nonsense, I had to creep out after he had gone to bed."

"You will not have to do that now," the Earl said.

She gave him a quick look which he did not understand.

He thought perhaps she doubted that he would keep his word.

With a final pat on *Firefly*'s neck she let the groom lead him away.

Then she went into the Castle with *Rufus* at her heels.

There were several other rooms which the Earl wanted to show her which she appeared to find fascinating.

She was very sympathetic when he showed her the empty spaces on the wall from which his Uncle had taken pictures or mirrors.

There was one room from which a number of Dresden porcelain figures had been taken and sold.

"You will have to replace them," Ansella said.

"I hope that will by your job," the Earl answered.

"Mine?" Ansella questioned.

"Of course," he said. "If we do things properly, you will run the house and make it as beautiful as you can. I will cope with the Estate, and that is going to take quite a long time."

He was thinking when he spoke that from what he had seen already he would have to spend all the money Lord Frazer had given him.

This meant he would soon have to ask for more.

He knew it would be humiliating to have to do so.

Yet if he was ever to restore the place to what it had been in his Father's day, it would take both time and money.

He wondered why he should have to cope with two such unpleasant men as his Uncle and Lord Frazer.

"You are . . . looking . . . cross," he heard a nervous little voice say beside him. "Have I . . . done something . . . wrong?"

"No, of course not," the Earl replied. "I was just feeling rather bitter over losing possessions that my Mother had collected over many years. Just as I am wondering what I shall ride if I have to keep up with *Firefly*."

"You mean you want to . . . buy a . . . horse?" Ansella enquired.

"I most certainly do," the Earl replied. "But I think it wrong, when there is so much to be done here, that I should go to London to Tattersall's Sales, which I expect you know take place every week."

Ansella thought for a moment, and then she said:

"I remember a week or two ago Papa had a letter from a man called Tyler, who has a very fine stable."

"Tyler!" the Earl said. "I seem to have heard of him."

"Papa bought horses from him recently which were outstanding, and when he wrote to Papa he said he had several very good hunters. However, Papa said he had enough to last him through the winter. I think he was aware that I might not be with him."

'That was,' the Earl thought, 'just when I was returning home and Lord Frazer was counting his chickens and thinking that here was the Bridegroom he wanted for his daughter. There would therefore be no need for any more horses for the coming winter.'

*100*

"What you have told me is very interesting and important," he said aloud. "I will send someone over to Tyler's house which I think is only two or three miles from here and ask him to show me the horses he offered your Father."

"That is a good idea," Ansella said, "but hurry in case someone else buys them first."

The Earl laughed.

He told Marlow to send a groom over to Tyler's Stables immediately.

By this time the horse that had taken the Accountant back to Oxford should have returned.

Otherwise the man must ride the one which had just come from Watton Hall.

"Now you will have to help me choose something to ride that is as good as *Firefly*," the Earl said to Ansella.

"No one could be better than him," she said, "but perhaps we can find one which is nearly as good."

The Earl laughed.

"You are quite right to support your own choice," he said. "But I really cannot be left behind when we go riding or have a horse that funks a fence."

Ansella smiled at this.

He thought it made her look lovely.

It was a pity she should look so sad and frightened as she had ever since he had known her.

It was soon time for tea, and Marlow had it all ready in the Drawing-Room.

It was a relief to the Earl to see that the George III silver had not been sold as he had feared it might have been.

Mrs. Marlow had managed to get ingredients for some sandwiches and small cakes besides the Wedding-Cake.

"Now you have to eat something," the Earl said to Ansella, "otherwise you will get so thin you will waste away, or be blown off the Tower by the wind."

"I will try," she promised.

She did manage to eat a certain amount.

Then the Earl said:

"Now I am going to insist that you lie down before dinner. I think if you are sensible you will try to sleep. Is your back still hurting?"

"Not like it did before," she answered.

"Then go and lie down," he said. "I will take *Rufus* for a walk, but I expect he would rather be with you."

The Earl noticed that she had furtively fed him with little pieces of cake.

She had done it when she thought he was not looking.

He guessed her Father had forbidden her to feed the dog just because it had made her happy to do so.

'I must have some dogs about me too,' the Earl thought.

He decided he would ask Cosnat, who had always had a dog with him, where he could obtain two sporting dogs already well-trained.

When Ansella had obediently gone up to bed, he went out into the garden and then down to the lake.

The evening sun was still warm.

The rooks were going to roost in the oak trees.

He was thinking he must have stags back in the park, Swans on the lake, and also a few ducks.

They would attract others that were wild and it would soon look as it had in the past.

He walked for quite a long way.

It aroused memories of what he had seen and where he had been in the past.

It was only when he returned to the house that he remembered it was his wedding-night.

He had hoped by this time that Ansella would somehow have stopped being frightened.

He could understand with her Father's appalling cruelty she had been frightened not only of him but of men, and that included himself.

'I must be very gentle with her,' he thought.

It was something he had never had to think about with a woman before.

For a moment he felt she was just a frightened child whom he somehow had to defend and comfort.

'She is very young,' he thought. 'At the same time definitely intelligent.'

He had been surprised at her interest in books, but he realised now that they were in a way the only companions she had had.

It seemed strange that Lord Frazer had not entertained for her in any way.

He gathered she had not been to any Balls or Dances since she was eighteen.

Thinking it over, the Earl decided it was because of his obsession that his daughter should have a grand Society Wedding.

Lord Frazer had been afraid to let her mix with ordinary young men with whom she might fall in love.

He was not liked in the County, so his neighbours did not invite him to their houses.

Thinking it over carefully, the Earl was certain that Lord Frazer had always been aware of the importance of the Earls of Rayburne.

When his Father died, he had perhaps then decided that if possible, he would marry his daughter to his next-door neighbour.

When the Viceroy had been murdered, it must have seemed to Lord Frazer that fate was playing into his hands, especially since the Earl would come home to penury.

It was almost like a story in a novel unfolding itself in front of him.

It infuriated him to think that he had been used like a pawn in the hand of a very clever player.

Then he told himself that however angry it made him, he must not let it affect his behaviour towards Ansella.

Whether he liked it or not, she was his wife.

As his wife, he must treat her with respect and make her eventually take her rightful place as *Châtelaine* of the Castle.

It was not going to be easy, he knew that.

He thought that if the Viceroy had been in his place, he would somehow have found a solution to the whole problem.

The first problem was to stop Ansella from being so frightened.

'I have every reason to be grateful to her,' the Earl decided as he walked back home.

Therefore, somehow he had to make her happy.

She had certainly looked very much happier since her dog and horse arrived.

"We must have some more of both," the Earl murmured.

He walked into the Courtyard and up the steps to the front door.

He went straight upstairs to his bedroom.

Marlow was there putting out his evening-clothes.

With him was a young man he was training to Valet the Earl and any other Gentlemen who came to stay at the Castle.

"It is a lovely evening, Marlow," the Earl said as he entered his bedroom.

" 'Tis, M'Lord, an' a happy day for all of us. I sent to the village an' got a great deal of the things the Missus required for dinner, an' her's very happy to have 'em."

The Earl smiled, and started to undress.

His bath was laid out on the usual place in front of the mantelpiece, although it was too warm to need a fire.

He certainly felt better when he had soaked in the warm water and rubbed himself down with a large Turkish towel.

When he was dressed in his evening-clothes he looked at himself in the mirror.

He thought he was smart enough to go to a Viceregal Reception, or, for that matter, a dinner at Buckingham Palace.

He had an impulse to tell Marlow as it was his wedding-night, he would put on a decoration he had received when he was in the Horse Guards.

Then he told himself that was being childish.

He went downstairs to the Drawing-Room.

He was not surprised to find the room empty, and there was no sign of Ansella.

It was getting on for eight o'clock when finally she came shyly through the door.

She was wearing a rather more elaborate gown than he had expected.

It was not white but a very pale green, the colour of Spring leaves.

It made her look almost like a sprite from the woods or a nymph from the lake.

"I am . . . sorry . . . I am . . . late," she said as she came towards him.

"You have two minutes to spare," the Earl replied. "And let me tell you, you look very charming in that pretty gown."

"I thought . . . perhaps you . . . would think . . . I should wear . . . white," she answered nervously. "But . . . this is one of my favourite dresses . . . because it makes me think of the . . . woods."

"Just as it made me think of them as you came through the door," the Earl said as he smiled.

"I love the woods," Ansella said, "but I do not like to think of them shooting the little rabbits or the birds."

The Earl thought it best not to answer this.

Instead, he said:

"Marlow tells me Mrs. Marlow has got a lot of ingredients we have not had for a long time. So be prepared for a feast to be waiting for you in the Dining-Room."

"Will she be very . . . disappointed if we do not . . . eat . . . a lot?" Ansella asked.

"Very," the Earl replied.

She made a helpless little gesture, and the Earl said:

"You can always slip what you do not eat under the table, where I know an open mouth will be waiting for it."

*Rufus* had followed Ansella into the room.

Now she looked first at the Earl and then at *Rufus*.

He knew that she was surprised that he had suggested such a thing.

After a moment she said:

"Papa was . . . very angry if I . . . fed *Rufus* when I was at . . . the table. But then, he did not . . . like him because he was . . . my dog."

"I am afraid my dogs have always looked for tit-bits from the table," the Earl replied, "and when I have some again, as I intend to do, *Rufus* will have to be quick or he will not get his share."

"I will see he does," Ansella said, "that is if you are not . . . angry with me for . . . feeding him."

"I can hardly be angry with you for something I am doing myself," the Earl said.

"Dinner is served, My Lady," Marlow said from the door.

The Earl offered Ansella his arm.

In the Dining-Room he was very touched to see that Cosnat, at Marlow's suggestion, had decorated the table with flowers.

They were mostly white and included some wild marigolds and even a few daisies.

It made the table look festive, and Ansella gave a little cry of delight.

"On our fiftieth anniversary," the Earl said, "we shall doubtless be able to have orchids, but tonight we have to be grateful for small mercies."

"I am very grateful to the person who thought of it," Ansella said, "and the flowers are very, very pretty."

The Earl knew that Marlow was pleased.

He hurried to bring in the dinner.

There were three courses, all beautifully cooked, just as Mrs. Marlow had managed in the past.

The Earl thought with satisfaction that things were really getting better.

Although he still had a long way to go, the first steps were certainly encouraging.

They talked through dinner of all the things he intended to do on the Estate.

He was aware that Ansella was listening wide-eyed.

"You will have to help me," he said. "I cannot do all this alone and, most important, you must get to know the people in the village who, of course, are very curious about you."

"Do . . . you think they will . . . hate me because I am . . . Papa's daughter?" Ansella asked.

The Earl shook his head.

"There is no reason for you to think that. You are now my wife, and as they have loved me ever since I was a small boy, they will love you because you belong to me."

He was not certain whether Ansella gave a little shiver when he said that or not.

"You must . . . tell me what . . . to do," she said humbly. "Papa never let me go into . . . our village except . . . in a carriage. If I wanted to shop, he would make me go to Oxford, where, of course, I knew nobody."

The Earl made no comment, but after a moment he said:

"You will find the village people here think they belong to the Castle. Therefore when my Father and Mother were alive, we tried to share with them their joys and their sorrows."

"I will . . . try to do . . . the same," Ansella murmured.

Because he had no wish to frighten her, the Earl then talked of other things.

He remembered that she had listened excitedly and intently to everything he had told her about India.

As he had also been to a great number of other places like Egypt, Greece, and, of course, France, he found himself delivering rather a monologue.

Yet no one could have had a more attentive audience.

When dinner was finished, they went into the Drawing-Room.

The Earl, feeling he had talked long enough, produced a Chess Board.

He thought this might have disappeared like a great many other things in the house.

"Marlow tells me he hid this away in the safe," he said, "so if you do not know Chess, I will teach you how to play it."

"I do know," Ansella said. "Papa liked to play Chess in the Winter evenings. He played with me and he was very annoyed if I won."

The Earl laughed.

"I will not be annoyed, but I shall certainly try to beat you."

The Chess Board was very old and the beautiful pieces were carved out of different types of marble.

It had been given to his Father many years ago and was, he knew, a treasure for its unique carvings.

They sat down on each side of a small table.

The Earl found that Ansella was a very good player.

In fact, only with great difficulty did he just manage to beat her.

"Checkmate!" he said with an air of triumph.

She clapped her hands as she said:

"You have won, you have really won! I tried very hard to beat you."

"We will play again another night," the Earl said.

He folded up the board and put it away in the drawer of one of the tables.

Then, when he turned round, he saw that Ansella was standing looking rather irresolute in front of the mantelpiece.

"You have had a long day," he said kindly. "I am sure you are very tired. Tomorrow morning we might go riding, although I feel that *Firefly* will outride the poor old horse that I am left with."

"Perhaps Mr. Tyler's horses ... will arrive ... before that," Ansella said.

"If he has not already sold them," the Earl remarked.

As he spoke, he walked towards the door, and after a second's pause, Ansella followed him.

He crossed the hall, where now only one of the footmen was on night duty.

Marlow had told him exactly what to do.

The chair on which he could sleep if he got the chance was beside the front door.

It was padded with a hood, and the Earl remembered it being there when he was a boy.

It was always the perquisite of the night-porter.

"Goodnight, James," the Earl said as they walked past him.

"Goodnight, M'Lord, goodnight, M'Lady," the footman replied.

They walked slowly up the stairs.

As they did so, the Earl was aware that once again Ansella was trembling.

They reached her bedroom door, and he opened it for her.

"I expect Mrs. Shepherd," he said, "has told you that she will come to help you undress if you need her."

He had remembered that he had said to Ansella that no one would see her back except the Housekeeper.

She would therefore not be expecting or wishing to have one of the maids.

"I told . . . Mrs. Shepherd that I can . . . manage," Ansella said.

"Are you quite sure you can?" the Earl asked.

She nodded.

Then, as she did not go into the room but just stood looking at him, he said:

"I can see you are worried about something, what is it?"

She looked away from him, then back at the stairs as if she were afraid the footman might overhear anything that she said.

The Earl walked into her bedroom.

There were lights on the Dressing-Table and one beside the bed.

It looked very attractive.

The Earl thought there was no need for her to feel that she should have had his Mother's room as was traditional.

Ansella had followed him into the room.

Now as he turned to look at her he realised fear was back in her eyes and she was still trembling.

"Now what is it?" he asked. "I thought we had a happy dinner together and you were no longer frightened as you were earlier today."

She did not answer, and he said after a moment:

"We did say we would have no secrets from each other, and I want you to tell me the truth. Do you dislike me so much that it makes you frightened when I am near you?"

"No . . . no . . . it is . . . not . . . that," Ansella replied.

"Then what is it?" he enquired.

She was twisting her fingers together and she looked away from him almost as if she wanted to run and hide.

"Please tell me, Ansella," he said coaxingly.

"Papa . . . said," Ansella said in a whisper he could hardly hear, "that . . . you were . . . going to do . . . something to ... me tonight and I was ... not to ... make a ... fuss."

The words seemed to come out jerkily from her lips.

The Earl felt it difficult for a moment to think of an answer.

He had known from the moment he had married her that Ansella was very innocent, which was to be expected in a young girl.

He could also understand that where she was concerned, having been treated so brutally by her Father and having no idea what marriage meant, she was terrified of the unknown.

'It is typical of Lord Frazer,' the Earl thought, 'to frighten her without explaining the reason for it.'

With an effort he tried to think how the Viceroy would have coped in such a situation and knew the answer.

"I expect," he said lightly, "your Father meant I would kiss you, but I think you have forgotten something."

"What ... is ... that?" Ansella asked still in a whisper.

"We have only just been introduced to each other, I think it was at tea-time, and I could hardly be expected to say 'how do you do, Miss Frazer,' and then kiss you."

"That would ... seem a ... little ... strange," Ansella admitted.

Now there was a faint smile on her lips.

"Very strange indeed," the Earl replied. "So you must not expect me to do anything like that until we know each other very well. In fact, not until you want me to kiss you."

His voice was very quiet.

"I was ... only ... frightened," she said, "that I ... should do ... something ... wrong and ... you would be ... angry."

"I think, and this is the truth, Ansella," the Earl said, "that I would find it extremely difficult to be angry with you. Just think of me as someone you have met who finds you very pretty, very intelligent, and is eager to get to know you better."

As she did not answer, he said quickly:

"Of course, as we are not married, have only just been introduced, and are staying alone in the Castle, you must have a chaperon. He is a relative and his name is *Mr. Rufus* and I am sure he will chaperon you most competently."

It was then Ansella laughed.

It was the first time he had heard her laugh, and it was a very pretty sound.

"Of course *Rufus* can chaperon me," she said. "I will tell him to . . . bite anyone who is . . . unkind to . . . me."

"You do exactly that," the Earl said.

He bent down and patted *Rufus*, who licked his hand.

"Now, Ansella," he said, "go to bed and dream happy dreams of all the exciting things we are going to do together."

He stood up, then bent down to pat *Rufus* again.

"Look after her," he said, "and bite anyone who comes into the bedroom after I have gone."

Ansella gave another little laugh.

"I am sure he will do that," she said, "and thank you for . . . being so . . . kind to . . . me."

The Earl took her hand.

"Goodnight, Ansella."

He gently raised her hand to his lips, then walked towards the door.

He did not look back, but he had the idea Ansella was watching until he was completely out of sight.

# *chapter six*

THE horses went quicker and quicker until just ahead of them there was a stream.

The Earl pulled in his mount and Ansella did the same.

As she did so, she looked up at him, laughing.

"That was wonderful!" she exclaimed. "I think *Star* goes faster every time you ride him!"

The Earl bent to pat the stallion on the neck and thought as he did so, it had been an excellent buy.

Following Ansella's information, he had seen Tyler's horses and could not resist buying four of them.

He excused the extravagance because he thought if they rode every day as far as they had been doing lately, *Firefly* would occasionally want a rest.

Looking at Ansella now, he thought the difference in her from her condition a week ago was extraordinary.

Instead of the frightened, trembling girl he had married, she was now laughing with him.

She found, as he did, that every day was a new adventure.

He had never imagined a woman being as excited as he was at the refurbishing of the Castle.

But the new developments on the Estate and the restoration of the village thrilled her.

One of the first things he had done was to apply for a new Vicar.

The Bishop, who had obviously been shocked by his Uncle's behaviour, sent a very nice man whom both he and Ansella liked on sight.

He was married with three children, and he wanted a quiet living because he was writing a book.

He had already moved into the Vicarage, and the Earl and Ansella had occupied the family pew on Sunday.

The Earl was also considering opening a School.

They had long discussions with Joe Higgins and some of the older men and women in the village as to how it could be managed.

There were, the Earl found, a great number of young children who needed schooling and whose education had been completely neglected up to now.

He found arranging all this very much like his work with the Viceroy in India.

There they had to set up Schools, Hospitals, and many other public services wherever they went.

What did surprise him was the interest that Ansella took in all this.

He realised it was because she had never been allowed to take part in any of her Father's activities.

Therefore she had never come in contact with ordinary people.

At first she was rather shy.

Then, when she found they wanted to tell her their difficulties, their sorrows, and their joys, she listened attentively and was very sympathetic.

She looked so lovely now.

Her hair was blown from the speed at which they had been galloping into little curls round her cheeks, which were flushed into a soft pink.

As he smiled at her, he thought that if he kissed her skin, it would be like touching satin.

It was something he had thought of before.

Last night he had wondered if he could go to her bedroom to talk to her before she went to sleep.

He knew, to be honest, that he wanted to kiss her and find out if she was still afraid of him.

But he told himself it was too soon.

He must be very careful not to bring back the terror into her eyes.

He remembered all too vividly how she had trembled at first when he went near her.

He knew that he had to be very patient and wait until she fell in love with him.

He could not believe that of all the women in the world she would be the only one who was not attracted to him.

But he had to admit to himself that she treated him in the same way she might have treated her brother if she had one.

She took an intense interest in everything he said and everything he did.

At the same time, he did not feel that in her eyes he was an attractive man.

'I have got to wait,' he told himself. But it was proving to be rather harder than he expected.

Now they crossed the stream where it was shallow.

When they reached the other side they passed through some trees and then began to climb.

The Earl had told Ansella about the statue which had been erected to his Great Grandfather on the top of the hill at one end of the Estate.

"I would love to see it," she said.

"We will ride there," he replied, "and I think you will find it interesting, as my Great Grandfather designed it himself. It is very different from the usual statues that are erected in this part of the country."

They had set off that morning after breakfast.

Because they were going such a long way, the Earl had said *Rufus* must stay behind.

"It would be too much for him," he said, "and of course for my dogs also."

He had bought two Spaniels for himself and Ansella had been delighted with them.

She did not think they were as beautiful as *Rufus*, because that would be impossible.

The three dogs got on together very well.

They followed their owners obediently wherever they went.

"I hate leaving *Rufus* behind," Ansella said as they rode away from the Stables.

"I can understand that," the Earl said. "At the same time, it does the dogs good to have a rest, and they were quite a long way with us yesterday."

Ansella had to acknowledge this was true.

Then she said aloud:

"You are very kind to your animals, and when I came to live at the Castle I never thought I would be allowed to have *Rufus* with me."

The Earl did not comment because he disliked speaking about Lord Frazer.

He knew too that the less Ansella thought about her Father, the better.

Now, as the ground was steeper, they had to go even more slowly.

There were more trees, then some bushes.

Finally, just ahead of them they could see the statue of the Earl's Great Grandfather.

It was certainly very impressive.

He had been a soldier and he had been sculpted wearing his uniform.

He stood looking out over the broad acres he had owned.

He was, Ansella thought, far larger and taller than she had expected.

It was only as they drew nearer that she realised the statue was not standing on an ordinary base.

The base, in fact, appeared to be almost like a small house or a rather elaborate shed.

The Earl realised she was puzzled.

"This will surprise you," he said. "My Great Grandfather felt pity for people having to climb up this steep hill to admire him. So he provided them with somewhere they could sit and rest and, I suspect, eat anything like sandwiches they had brought with them."

He dismounted as he spoke and tied his reins on the top of *Star*'s back.

Ansella was doing the same to *Firefly*.

The Earl then looked at his horse a little warily.

"Wicks assured me," he said, "that *Star* has been trained to come when one whistles and not to move away too far from where he is left."

"I have trained *Firefly* to do that," Ansella said.

"Yes, I know," the Earl replied. "But you have had *Firefly* for a long time and I am taking rather a risk with *Star*. I have no wish to walk home."

Ansella laughed.

"If the worse comes to the worst, you will have to ride *Firefly* with me or else I will go ahead to get help."

"That is certainly a consoling thought," the Earl replied.

They left the horses and went up a little further until they reached the building on which the statue stood.

The Earl lifted the heavy bar across the door.

Now Ansella could see there was a small room in which there was a table and several chairs.

Against one wall there was a cleverly constructed model of the Castle.

It had iron bars round it to prevent it from being taken away.

She looked at it with delight.

"It is beautifully made!" she exclaimed.

"It was given to my Great Grandfather by his Regiment when he retired," the Earl said, "and he was intensely proud of it. He had it put here so that more people could see it than would do so if it were kept in the Castle itself."

"It is lovely," Ansella said, "and I think it was very kind of your Great Grandfather to provide these chairs and tables for people who, if they walked all the way up here, would be exhausted."

"I think we have very few visitors nowadays," the Earl said.

The place was certainly rather dusty.

Then he looked round and said:

"Now you will have to come outside to look at the statue of my Great Grandfather from every angle. He certainly wanted to be admired."

Ansella gave a little laugh.

"Are you going to erect a statue of yourself?" she asked.

"Certainly not," the Earl replied. "All I want to leave to posterity, when I can afford it, is a portrait of myself to add to the portraits of my ancestors, which you have not yet seen, in the Picture Gallery."

"Why have I not seen that?" Ansella asked.

"For the simple reason," the Earl replied, "that by great good fortune the floor of the Gallery needed repairing before I went away. I therefore had the pictures stored in a safe place."

He gave a little sigh of relief.

"If I had not done so," he finished, "I am quite certain that my Uncle would have sold a great number of them."

"Now you must get them back," Ansella said.

"We will do that as soon as we have time," the Earl replied.

Then, as he turned towards the door, he stopped still.

Three men had just come in from outside and were standing inside the small room, looking at him.

For a moment the Earl could hardly believe what he was seeing.

Each man was wearing dark glasses and had a black handkerchief over the lower part of his face.

All three had revolvers in their hands.

"Now, what is all this about?" he asked.

He thought, in fact, it was some joke.

It seemed a very strange one, especially as they were so far away from the village.

"We have come, My Lord," the man in the centre said, "to ask Your Lordship to sign a cheque that I have brought with me."

As he spoke, he walked towards the table.

The two men who had been on either side of him moved together to block the doorway.

"A cheque?" the Earl questioned. "Who are you?"

"That is immaterial," the man replied. "But I and my friends have heard of your generosity to the people in the villages on your Estate. So we feel we also are entitled to Your Lordship's consideration."

He was speaking in a mocking manner.

At the same time, the Earl was aware that he had an educated voice, although there was just a faintly common tinge in his accent.

From the way the three men were dressed, he was aware that they must have been riding.

As if he had asked the question, the man who had been speaking said:

"We followed you, and I must admit that it is exceedingly convenient that you can write your signature on a table rather than a stone, and I am providing you with the pen and ink to do so."

"I have already asked you," the Earl replied, "what all this is about and who you are."

"Shall I say," the man replied, "that we are prepared to be very grateful for Your Lordship's charity, and we are asking for a mere three thousand pounds from you. Under the circumstances, we could easily ask for more."

The Earl was aware what the circumstances were.

The two men in front of the door were still pointing their revolvers at him.

He also knew that Ansella was frightened.

She had moved closer to him, although she did not touch him or speak.

The man put the cheque down on the table and the Earl saw to his astonishment it was from his own Bank.

"How did you get hold of that?" he asked.

"That is my business," was the reply. "As Your Lordship can see, it is already made out for three thousand pounds, which is very much less than you are giving to those people who live in the shadow of your Castle. My colleagues and I thought it would be a mistake to be greedy."

What they really thought, the Earl knew, was that the Bank would cash his cheque for three thousand pounds, but if it was for any more, they would undoubtedly ask awkward questions.

There was silence, and then the Earl said:

"I cannot imagine that you really think I will do what you ask. The money I have given my employees does not concern you, and I need all I possess to carry out the improvements which are necessary for the comfort and well-being of those who rely on me."

"A very pretty speech," the man answered sneeringly. "At the same time, the sooner Your Lordship does what we ask, the quicker we can be on our way."

"I refuse," the Earl said quietly.

One of the men at the door made a sound like a chuckle.

The man who had been speaking said:

"You cannot expect me to take 'No' for an answer. Of course if Your Lordship requires an incentive to spur you into action, I could cut off Her Ladyship's pretty hair or perhaps the small finger from her left hand."

He was speaking sarcastically, but the Earl knew he meant what he said.

Ansella gave a little cry of horror.

Now she was holding on to his arm and the Earl could feel she was trembling.

"I find it difficult to submit to blackmail," he said bitterly, "but I suppose there is no alternative."

"None!" the man replied.

He held out the quill pen and the Earl took it from him.

There was a small bottle of ink which he had uncorked on the table beside the cheque.

It flashed through the Earl's mind that he might throw the ink into the Blackmailer's face and tear up the cheque.

Then he remembered the two men standing by the door with their revolvers in their hands.

He was helpless and he knew it.

He could not go on letting Ansella be as frightened as she was at that moment.

He took the pen which was held out to him.

For a moment he hesitated.

He knew if he signed his name in any way that was unusual the Bank would be suspicious.

As the Earl of Rayburne it was correct for him to sign with the name of his title.

He thought if he put Michael Rayburne it might make the cheque invalid.

The man watching him, however, knew what he was thinking.

"It would be a mistake, My Lord," he said, "to do anything which would annoy me, and it would certainly upset Her Ladyship, who would find what I did to her very painful."

The Earl signed his name correctly.

When he had done so, the Blackmailer picked the cheque up and waved it backwards and forwards in his hand so as to dry the ink.

Then he said:

"That is extremely satisfactory."

As he spoke, Ansella gave a little scream, and the Earl felt a rope being thrown round his chest.

It took the three men only a few minutes to bind his arms and legs with a rope.

They then did the same to Ansella.

Then they set them down with their backs to the wall and walked towards the door.

"I am afraid it may be some time," the spokesman said, "before Your Lordship is rescued. Unless, of course, as it is a nice day, some sight-seers climb up to look at your ancestor. If, however, none arrive, I can only hope that you will be more fortunate tomorrow."

There was the same jeering note in his voice he had used when they first arrived.

When he finished speaking, the two men with him walked out through the door and he followed them.

The door was pushed to and the Earl heard the heavy bar fall into place.

For a moment neither he nor Ansella spoke.

Then she said in a frightened little voice:

"What are . . . we . . . going . . . to do?"

"We have to try to release ourselves," the Earl said, speaking as calmly as he could, "and I can only apologise for bringing you here."

122

"How could . . . you know . . . how could . . . you have guessed . . . those terrible men . . . would appear?"

"I cannot understand it," the Earl said. "How was it possible for them to get hold of one of my cheques?"

He was really talking to himself, but Ansella said:

"We have . . . to escape . . . we cannot stay here . . . perhaps no one will . . . find us and . . . we shall . . . just die."

"That will not happen," the Earl said. "If we do not return, Wicks knew where we were going and will undoubtedly come to look for us."

Ansella gave a little sigh.

"I did . . . not think . . . of that."

"All the same, it is infuriating," the Earl said, "to let those Devils get away with it. If we can get free, we can send the Police looking for them before they can cash my cheque."

"I expect they . . . will go . . . straight to . . . Oxford and cash it long . . . before we can . . . get there," Ansella said.

The Earl did not answer, and after a moment she went on:

"I was . . . frightened . . . very frightened, but they did not gag . . . us and it is . . . comforting to be . . . able to . . . talk to . . . you."

"I am determined to stop them if I can," the Earl asserted.

He thought for a moment, and then he said:

"The best thing I can do is to try to undo your hands. Can you turn sideways?"

The men had pulled her arms back and tied her hands behind her.

They had also bound her legs and ankles together.

She was not only uncomfortable but completely helpless.

They had done the same to the Earl but using more rope.

It was with the greatest difficulty he managed to turn towards her.

He saw rope ends sticking out above her wrists and said:

"I am going to try to set your hands free. I am afraid it may take time, as I have no wish to break my teeth."

"How can...you possibly...do that?" Ansella asked. "The rope is...very thick."

"We cannot just sit here waiting and let those men get away with it," the Earl said. "They have made me look a fool, and that is something I shall not forget in a hurry."

He thought how in India he and the Viceroy had always carried revolvers.

Yet how could he have imagined that he would need one in the quiet countryside of his own Estate in England?

He was furious at finding himself helpless against three armed Blackmailers.

He was therefore determined, if it was humanly possible, to prevent them from getting away with the money he needed so urgently.

It took him some time to get into a position where he could work on the rope which held Ansella's wrists and hands together.

Eventually he managed it.

He was aware when his lips touched the rope it was not as rough or as hard as he had feared.

The Blackmailers carried it with them because it was effective for what they wanted.

It was not, however, the very coarse type which was used on ships.

As he said to Ansella, he had no wish to break his teeth.

It was a difficult task to bite away the rope until finally, nearly an hour later, Ansella gave a cry.

"You have done it!" she exclaimed as she pulled her arms free.

The Earl raised himself back against the wall.

He thought of all the many different things he had done in his life, this had been the most difficult.

It did not take her long to unfasten the rope tied round her legs and ankles.

As she did so, she was moving her fingers, her hands, and her arms, which had become numb.

Then she said:

"Now I must free you, and I am glad I can use my fingers instead of my teeth."

It took her some time, because the rope had been tied very tightly, to release the Earl's hands from behind his back.

Eventually she managed it, and he was now able to free his legs and ankles.

He stood up, moving around to restore the circulation to his limbs, and she watched him anxiously.

"Are you all right?" she asked.

He smiled at her.

"Perfectly, except I have cramps in my legs."

He stamped on the floor, and then he said:

"Now there is another problem, how are we going to get out?"

Ansella had not thought of this, but she had seen how the door was barred.

She knew however hard they pushed, there was no chance of moving it.

The Earl looked round.

The small room was ventilated by two long, narrow windows, which also let in the light.

They reached to the ceiling but were only a few inches in breadth.

Ansella followed the direction of his eyes and said:

"They are very narrow, but I think perhaps I can climb through them."

The Earl stared at her in astonishment.

"I am sure that is impossible."

"We have to try," Ansella insisted.

She thought he was about to refuse her and said aloud:

"How can we sit here meekly, hoping that it will not be too long before Wicks sends a search party for us? He might think he was interfering and do nothing."

The Earl looked at the window again.

"You are small," he said, "but it would be very difficult to wriggle through that narrow space."

"I am determined to try," Ansella said.

Then she paused and was silent.

"What are you thinking?" the Earl asked. "Have you changed your mind?"

She did not answer for a moment. Then she stammered:

"I have only . . . just realised I . . . will have . . . to take off my . . . riding-habit."

The Earl could not help smiling.

He thought how many women had been only too willing to undress in front of him.

Yet now his wife was shy.

He liked her modesty because it was what he expected of her.

He thought for a moment, and then he said:

"I tell you what I will do. I will have to lift you up to the window, but I promise I will shut my eyes, and you will have to direct me."

"That is clever of you," Ansella said, "and I only . . . hope there is . . . not anyone . . . watching from . . . outside."

"If there is," the Earl said practically, "he or she can go and open the door."

"Yes . . . of course," Ansella agreed, "I had not . . . thought of . . . that."

The Earl turned his back towards her.

"Tell me when you are ready for me to turn round."

Ansella took off her riding-jacket and skirt.

As the weather was warm, she was wearing very little underneath.

She could not help giving some anxious little glances towards the Earl as she undressed.

He did not move, and finally, when she had taken off her riding-boots, she said in a small voice:

"I am ready . . . now but . . . please do not . . . look."

"My eyes are tightly shut," the Earl replied.

He turned round and put out his hands towards her.

He had already opened the window before she undressed.

He still thought it would be quite impossible for Ansella to squeeze out of it however optimistic she might be.

He picked her up and was aware how light she was, just as he had thought when he had first carried her when she had fainted after their Wedding.

Now he could feel the softness of her skin.

He thought without her clothes she would look even more like a Goddess from Olympus than she had in her simple gowns.

"I must go out feet first," Ansella said, "so that I can . . . hold on to . . . you until I . . . slip down . . . on the ground."

Once again the Earl thought she was being optimistic.

He lifted her so that her feet went through the window, then her knees.

It was then she began to wriggle.

He thought although she was doing it very skilfully, edging one way and then another, it would be impossible to get her whole body through the narrow window.

Then suddenly her behind was through.

She was suspended by her waist with half of her outside and the other half holding on to the Earl on the inside.

"I think . . . I can do . . . it," Ansella said with a note of triumph.

It was then the Earl opened his eyes.

She was not aware of it because she was looking backwards at the window.

He had a glimpse of her pale gold hair.

Her breasts were partially hidden by a lace-trimmed vest.

He felt the blood begin to throb in his temples.

He knew no one could be more lovely or more desirable, even at that moment.

Then, as he moved closer to the wall, Ansella twisted her shoulders through the window.

Finally taking her hands from the Earl, she held on to the ledge and dropped to the ground.

"I have . . . done it! I have . . . done it!" she cried. "I will . . . go and open . . . the door."

She ran round the side of the building and the Earl had a glimpse of her in the sunshine.

The next minute he could hear her heaving at the bar over the door.

A few seconds later it opened.

"Do not look!" she cried.

Obediently the Earl shut his eyes.

It was, however, not until he had seen her looking exquisitely lovely with the sun making her seem as if she had come down from Heaven itself.

She ran past the Earl and started to put on her clothes.

Because he knew it was the right thing to do, he went to the door and whistled for the horses.

He was half afraid the Blackmailers might have taken them with them.

Then he thought it unlikely because they were so distinctive.

Anyone seeing three men leading two such superlative horses would not only wonder where they had come from but, if there was an enquiry, would remember them.

By the time Ansella came out to join him and to whistle for *Firefly*, they could see the horses a little way down the hill.

*Firefly* raised his head, then trotted up towards them.

There was no sign of *Star*, but the Earl went on whistling.

Finally he came from behind the trees.

He seemed reluctant to climb the hill.

The Earl closed the door of what had been their prison, then walked down beside Ansella, who was mounted on *Firefly*.

Only when they were riding on the level ground in the direction of the Castle did he say:

"I cannot believe this has happened to us, or that you have been so exceedingly clever as to free us when I did not think there was the slightest chance of you being able to do so."

"Papa always laughed at me for being skinny," Ansella replied, "but I would never have got through that window if I had been even an ounce or two fatter."

"You were very clever and very brave," the Earl said. "I shall have to think of a medal I can give you."

With a faint smile he thought that most women he had known would have said what they wanted was him to kiss them.

Ansella replied:

"If you want to give me a present, *Rufus* needs a new collar."

"Then he shall have one," the Earl said, "but people would think it a little ostentatious if it was decorated with diamonds."

Ansella laughed.

"Is that what you want to give me?"

"It is what I would *like* to give you," the Earl said, "to show how grateful I am, but for the moment we cannot afford it."

"Not now that we have lost three thousand pounds," Ansella replied. "How dare those wicked men take our money!"

The Earl did not reply.

He was trying to think of some way of reaching the Bank before the Blackmailers.

They had spent a long time under his Great Grandfather's statue.

In fact, when he looked at his watch he found it was nearly three o'clock.

They had missed their luncheon.

Actually that they were hungry had never occurred to them, as they had been so intent on escaping.

'The Banks close at three,' the Earl reminded himself.

He thought angrily of what he could have bought in the way of seed or cattle with three thousand pounds.

They rode on quickly and almost in silence until the Castle came in sight.

"I want you to go to lie down," the Earl said to Ansella. "This has frightened you and has been a great strain. It would be sensible to rest while you have the chance."

"I will go and . . . change my . . . clothes," Ansella replied, "but I do not . . . want to rest, I want to . . . help you catch those . . . wicked thieves."

"I will try," the Earl said, "but I am afraid we do not have much hope now of stopping them cashing the cheque."

"How could they have got one of your cheque forms?" Ansella asked.

"I have no idea," the Earl answered, "unless they stole it or bribed someone in the Castle to give it to them. But I cannot imagine one of my people doing such a thing."

"Neither can I," Ansella said. "They all love you, and not one of them would do anything to hurt you."

They reached the Castle.

The three dogs were waiting for them in the hall and came rushing down the steps, barking loudly, to greet them.

They made such a noise that two grooms came running from the Stables to take the horses.

As they walked into the hall, Ansella said:

"I will not be long."

She ran upstairs with *Rufus* following her.

The Earl went towards his Study.

He was thinking, after all they had been through, he would ask Marlow to bring him a drink.

Then, just as he reached it, the Butler came hurrying down the passage behind him.

"I'm sorry, M'Lord," he said, "but I didn't hear you return. There's someone at the other door who wishes to see Your Lordship."

"Who is it, Marlow?" the Earl asked.

He had no wish to see someone from the village at that moment.

"It's someone from the Chief of Police, M'Lord," Marlow replied.

The Earl stared at him.

He was just thinking the best thing he could do was to get in touch with the Chief Constable.

"Send him in at once!" he ordered.

It took Marlow only a few moments to bring in a man whom the Earl recognised as one of the senior Police Officers in Oxford.

He had met him before he went abroad and fortunately remembered his name.

"This is a surprise, Mr. Johnson," he said, "although I was, in fact, going to ask you to come to see me immediately."

"I'm afraid, M'Lord," the Police Officer replied, "I have rather bad news."

"Bad news?" the Earl questioned.

"It concerns Lord Frazer," the Police Officer answered.

"What has happened?" the Earl enquired.

He sat down at his desk and indicated a chair in front of him.

"We've been searching," the Police Officer began, "for three men who have been holding up small shops in Oxford and taking money from them at pistol-point."

The Earl stiffened, but he did not say anything.

"This morning, I believe it was just after midday, they entered Watton Hall by a side window and confronted Lord Frazer, who was sitting alone at his desk in the Study."

"They were demanding money?" the Earl enquired.

"That is what I imagine they did," the Officer answered, "but unlike the shop-keepers who were obliged to hand over what they had, Lord Frazer drew a loaded revolver from a drawer, shot one man, and wounded another."

The Earl made an exclamation but did not speak, and the Police Officer went on:

"The third man shot at Lord Frazer."

"Did he kill him?" the Earl asked.

The Police Officer shook his head.

"No, he wounded him in the arm, but when the servants came running to see what was happening, His Lordship had a stroke."

"What has happened now?" the Earl asked.

"I came to see you, M'Lord," the Police Officer said, "because this was found in the pocket of the dead man."

He drew out the Earl's cheque as he spoke and put it down on the desk.

The Earl told him quickly what had happened earlier in the day and how he had intended to send for the Police.

"You were very wise, M'Lord, not to make any resistance," the Police Officer said. "Now all the men are in our hands and the two who are alive will undoubtedly get a very long prison sentence."

"How bad is Lord Frazer?" the Earl enquired.

"I'll be frank with Your Lordship," the Officer answered. "The Doctors who examined him think his stroke is a serious one. As Your Lordship knows, he may, however, linger for some time."

The Earl thought for a moment. Then he said:

"I am sure it would be a great mistake for there to be any publicity over this. I hope you will prevent it."

"We'll certainly do our best, and there is no reason why anything should be known of it until the men are brought before the Court."

"That is what I hoped," the Earl said. "My wife, who has been through a very unpleasant experience, need not be told of her Father's illness."

"I will make sure, M'Lord," the Police Officer said, "she is not informed of it until later. As you understand, His Lordship is at the moment unconscious and could not recognise anyone."

The Earl nodded.

Then he shook the Police Officer's hand, saying:

"Thank you for coming to see me, and of course I am available to give you any further information you require."

"I'll not bother Your Lordship unless it is necessary," he Police Officer promised.

When he had gone, the Earl walked to the window to look out at the sunshine.

He could hardly believe he and Ansella had been through this strange drama.

Yet, incredibly, his cheque had been returned to him.

He was certain that the Police would keep as quiet as possible about the whole proceedings.

As they had not been able to apprehend the men until they had caused so much trouble, it was not entirely to their credit.

'I am not going to tell Ansella about her Father,' the Earl thought, 'not at the moment. Not when she has only just recovered from being so frightened of him and incidentally of me. I have to protect her and I am sure this is the best way of doing it.'

He was speaking to himself.

When Ansella came into the room, she was smiling.

"I have been as quick as I could," she said. "What have you been doing?"

"Look on my desk," the Earl said.

She did so, and when she saw the cheque she gave a little cry.

"Your cheque! How did you get it back?"

"We were very lucky," the Earl said. "The Blackmailer who made me sign it has had an accident."

"And someone who found him brought back your cheque," Ansella said. "Oh, how lucky, how very, very lucky! I am so glad!"

"So am I," the Earl said, "and now we can just relax and not worry about anything except that I am very hungry."

"Now that I think of it, I am hungry too," Ansella said. "Dare we ask for anything substantial in the middle of the afternoon?"

"Well, I intend to have eggs for my tea," the Earl said, "and they will sustain me until it is dinner time."

"That is a lovely idea," Ansella exclaimed. "Marlow is in the hall. I will go and tell him that is what we want."

She did not wait for the Earl to reply or suggest they ring the bell, but ran down the passage.

As she did so, the Earl admitted to himself that he had fallen in love.

He loved her and he wanted her.

But he told himself very firmly he must not be in a hurry.

He had to wait.

# *chapter seven*


HEN the Earl went up to dress for dinner, he thought
had been a long day.

So much had happened and he still had so much to
ink about.

After breakfast he and Ansella had gone riding on two
 the new horses he had bought from Tyler.

He was eager for her to forget what had happened
vo days ago and he thought the new horses would be
 least a distraction.

Riding them for the first time was not only interesting,
it it also meant the horses had to realise from the be-
nning that he and Ansella were their Masters.

They rode for a long way, and he thought the coun-
yside had never looked more attractive.

The sunshine turned the leaves on the trees to gold
d the fields were brilliant with wild flowers.

He was well aware they should have been carrying
ops, but that was to come later.

It had rained just before dawn and there were dew drops on the grass and more water in the stream.

When they turned for home, Ansella said:

"That was a beautiful ride, and I am very thrilled with this horse. Are you pleased with yours?"

"Delighted!" the Earl said. "It was worth every penny."

"That is what I was thinking," Ansella said. "I am sure it is a mistake to worry too much about money."

The Earl agreed.

At the same time, he knew that money would be continual worry to him until he could pay back what he owed to Lord Frazer.

There was, of course, he knew at the back of his mind the chance that Lord Frazer would die from his stroke.

Somehow, despite what the Police Officer had said, since he was not yet sixty, he would probably live for long time.

Then, because it always depressed him, he tried to dismiss the thought of money from his mind.

When they got near the Castle, Ansella said:

"I do not know if you want me this afternoon, but Mrs. Shepherd had asked me to go with her to Oxford to buy some new sheets."

As the Earl did not answer, she said quickly:

"Of course Mrs. Shepherd could buy them alone, but I thought you would wish me to show I was taking an interest."

"Of course I wish you to do that," the Earl replied, "and I think it is an excellent idea. I will order a carriage and it will not take you long."

"I will be back for tea," Ansella said. "I am sure you will have something important to do."

"Too much," the Earl replied.

They had an excellent luncheon and then the Earl saw Ansella and Mrs. Shepherd off in the carriage.

He thought as they drove away that this was an excellent opportunity for him to go to see what was happening at Watton Hall.

It would be difficult if Ansella was at home to conceal from her where he was going.

What was more, she might have insisted on coming with him.

He was determined that she should not be upset by learning what had happened to her Father.

The less she thought about him and the way he had treated her in the past, the better.

This was imperative for her new attitude towards life.

'She is changing every minute of every day,' the Earl thought, 'and at the same time growing even more beautiful and more desirable.'

He had lain awake last night thinking about her and found it hard to sleep.

He knew that he was falling more and more in love.

It was a very different love from what he had felt for the women with whom he had amused himself in India and previously in London.

Then there had been a fiery desire that was very enjoyable.

At the same time, it did not last.

It had faded away like flames in a fire.

Then inevitably there were just ashes with no reason to think about them again.

What he felt for Ansella was very different.

He wanted to protect her and prevent her from being frightened.

He wanted her to be a part of himself.

He knew that what he was feeling was the love men had sought from the beginning of time, usually to find it was out of reach.

'I love her,' he thought as he rode away from the Stable on *Star*.

He crossed the fields towards Monks Wood.

139

He passed through the wood, which he had alway thought was one of the most attractive he had ever seen

Most of the trees were tall and old.

There were also firs and a delightful cluster of whit Beeches which he had remembered since he was a boy

There was a pool in the middle of the wood which h had always thought was magic.

As he moved slowly on *Star* down the mossy path, h could hear the rabbits rustling in the undergrowth.

The little red squirrels were chattering at him as the ran along the boughs overhead.

Then he was on Lord Frazer's land, which was so di ferent from his own.

Everything was well cultivated and cared for and we advanced in its growth.

The hedges were clipped, and as he rode nearer to tl house he could see the garden was ablaze with flower

Yet, because over all this was the dark menace of i owner, the Earl stiffened as he drew up outside the fro door.

As if they had been expecting visitors, there was groom to take his horse and he walked into the hall.

"I want to see Mr. Barrett," he said to the Butler, ' he is available."

Mr. Barrett was Lord Frazer's Secretary.

He also had a great deal to do with the manageme of the Estate.

Lord Frazer rarely trusted anyone but himself.

He therefore found a manager more of an encu brance than a help.

Mr. Barrett was a middle-aged man with an habitu expression of anxiety on his face.

He came hurrying into the Study, where the But had taken the Earl.

"I thought you would be calling, My Lord," he sa "and I was hoping to see you."

"I came as soon as I could," the Earl replied. "How is His Lordship?"

Mr. Barrett shook his head.

"He is still unconscious. The Doctors who came this morning can do nothing for him."

"Do you think he will recover?" the Earl asked.

It was for him a question of importance, and he wanted to have a truthful answer.

Mr. Barrett looked round as if he were afraid someone was listening.

Then, lowering his voice, he said:

"If Your Lordship asks my opinion, I think there is little chance of Lord Frazer ever being himself again."

The Earl raised his eyebrows.

"What do the Doctors think?"

"They tried at first to be very optimistic, but have now admitted that if he does become conscious, it is unlikely that he would be normal."

"I am sorry to hear that," the Earl replied.

He was, of course, not the least sorry, but it was the polite thing to say.

Sitting down in a chair, he indicated the one next to it and said:

"Now we must discuss this, Mr. Barrett. If His Lordship is going to be ill for a long time or perhaps not in his right mind, who is to run the Estate?"

"I was thinking, My Lord," Mr. Barrett said tentatively, "it would have to be you."

It was what the Earl expected, but it was somewhat of a shock to hear it spoken aloud.

"I have seen His Lordship's Will," Mr. Barrett went on hastily. "I expect Your Lordship knows he has left everything he possesses to his daughter. But one could hardly expect Miss Ansella, as I have always called her, to run the Estate, especially as she is married to Your Lordship."

"I suppose you and I can manage it together," the Earl said slowly.

He saw the light come into Mr. Barrett's eyes.

He had been afraid that if the Earl took over, he would no longer require his services.

"You will have to tell me," the Earl went on, "exactly what is required. As of course you know, I have seen little of His Lordship's Estate, let alone had anything to do with it."

He paused, and then continued:

"I have seen only this morning that the fields are well cultivated and everything seems in order."

"His Lordship was a hard task-master," Mr. Barrett answered, "because he expected perfection and was very angry if he did not get it."

The way he spoke told the Earl that Barrett had suffered in almost the same way as Ansella, except that Lord Frazer was unlikely to have struck him.

One thing was very plain: if Lord Frazer's stroke was as bad as the Doctors feared, then he could no longer bully Barrett or anyone else or, most important of all, his daughter.

"I would like to see His Lordship," he said aloud, "but first I want to know if you have heard anything else from the Police about the men who assaulted him."

"Oh, yes, My Lord, I should have told you about it at once," Mr. Barrett said hastily. "The Police Officer was here this morning and he informed me that the man whom His Lordship shot dead was formerly a junior Clerk with the solicitors Mayfield, Meadow, and Boyd."

The Earl gave an exclamation.

"My Solicitors!"

"I thought perhaps they were," Mr. Barrett said, "and His Lordship also employed them."

The Earl was now aware how the Blackmailers could have obtained a cheque on his Bank and have it ready for him to sign.

They might perhaps have been intending to try the same trick on Lord Frazer.

"The man His Lordship wounded," Mr. Barrett was saying, "is still alive, but the Police Officer says the Doctors do not expect him to live, and the third man is being held in Custody."

"Well, that certainly disposes of them," the Earl remarked.

"The Police Officer told me," Mr. Barrett went on, 'that they have robbed a considerable number of shops and poor people in Oxford, and they have been trying to catch them for some time."

The Earl only hoped that when the third man came up for trial, there would be nothing said about him and Ansella, also as little as possible about Lord Frazer.

At any rate, it would all take time.

There was no need for him to hurry to tell Ansella of her Father's illness.

Mr. Barrett eagerly offered to show the Earl the wages-book and details of last month's expenditure on the Estate.

To please him, the Earl agreed but said first he would like to see Lord Frazer.

He was taken upstairs to a large and impressive bedroom where Lord Frazer lay in a huge four-poster bed draped with velvet curtains.

He was on his back with his eyes closed.

The Earl thought that when he was unconscious he looked no less unpleasant than when he had been up and well.

His lips were closed in a sharp line.

There was still something cruel and evil about his face.

His man-servant, who was obviously on duty inside the bedroom, said in a low voice:

"I assure Your Lordship I've done everything I could, but he's not moved or spoken since they carried him up here."

The way he spoke told the Earl that he too was frightened of his Master and that he might be accused of neglecting him.

"I am sure you have done everything possible," the Earl said. "A stroke like this can leave a man or a woman unconscious for a very long time."

He was thinking of one of his Mother's sisters who, following a stroke, had lingered for a year before she finally died.

"There's nothing more we can do," the Valet said.

He still spoke as if he were frightened and the Earl would accuse him of negligence.

To cheer the man up, he said:

"I can see that both His Lordship and the Doctor are very lucky to have you to take care of His Lordship and there is no need for them to worry about him."

The Valet was obviously pleased and walked ahead to open the bedroom door for the Earl.

As he passed through it, he said:

"Thank you, M'Lord, thank you. If there's anything can do for you or Her Ladyship, I'm always at your service."

"That is very kind of you," the Earl replied.

He walked down the stairs thinking he was glad he was not staying in Watton Hall, and even more glad that Ansella was now with him in the Castle.

He was quite certain that if she were alone here, she would have been terrified by her Father's illness and frightened that if he recovered, he would somehow blame her for what had happened.

The Earl felt the whole house was oppressive and somehow creepy.

Lord Frazer had made it a background for himself.

The Earl felt as if everything that was unpleasant in him was impregnated in the atmosphere.

144

The rooms seemed tainted with the cruelty and brutality that was so much a part of His Lordship's character.

As he stepped out into the sunshine he drew a deep breath.

He knew he wanted to leave as quickly as possible.

He had, because he was eager to get away, forgotten Mr. Barrett.

The Secretary came running after him, saying in his nervous voice:

"I have the books ready to show Your Lordship."

"How stupid of me," the Earl said, "I had forgotten about them."

He went back into the Study, looked at the books, which were extremely well-kept, and congratulated Mr. Barrett.

Fortunately it did not take long.

Then he said:

"I am going to rely on you to keep things going, as I can see you are doing already. So do not send for me unless it is absolutely necessary."

He thought Mr. Barrett looked somewhat surprised, and he went on:

"To tell you the truth, and this is for your ears alone, I have not informed Her Ladyship of her Father's illness because quite frankly I do not want her to come here, and I know she would feel it her duty to do so."

Mr. Barrett was looking even more surprised, and the Earl continued:

"You must be aware how much your Master frightened his daughter and in fact how unkind in every possible way he was to her."

"Yes! Yes, My Lord," Mr. Barrett murmured, "we all knew that, but there was nothing we could do."

"No, of course not!" the Earl replied. "But now Miss Insella is my wife and I have no intention of letting her be upset or, if it is possible ever again, frightened by he Father."

He spoke sternly, but he wanted Mr. Barrett to un derstand.

Then he continued:

"That is why I want you to send for me only if it absolutely necessary, and of course to talk as little a possible about His Lordship's condition outside th house. Bad news, as we all know, travels on the wind and bad news is what I have no wish for Her Ladyshi to have at this moment."

"I understand," Mr. Barrett said, "and I promise yo My Lord, I will carry out your instructions and mak sure everyone in the house keeps their mouth shut."

"Thank you, Barrett, that is exactly what I want yo to do," the Earl said. "Carry on as you see best, I kno I can trust you."

The man was overcome that the Earl was so graciot to him.

He walked with his back to the front door.

He bowed as the Earl shook his hand and bowe again when having mounted *Star*, the Earl raised h hand before he rode off.

As the Earl went down the drive, he thought, if not ing else, he had left one person in Watton Hall happy

Instead of going back by Monks Wood, he thought would ride through the village.

He wanted to see if the men had already started r pairing the roofs and painting the cottages.

He was not disappointed.

There were quite a number of men doing exactly wh he had told them to do.

He thought it would not be long before the villa looked again as it had in his Father's day.

Then, when he had almost reached the lodge gates, saw Wicks in the driving seat of his carriage outside o of the cottages.

146

He rode up to it, realising before Wicks told him that Ansella and Mrs. Shepherd were inside.

The footman who had accompanied Ansella to Oxford jumped down from the box to hold *Star*.

The Earl walked up the cobbled path.

The door was open, and as he heard voices, he went in without knocking.

Ansella was standing in the centre of the room, and the Earl saw she was holding a baby in her arms.

For a moment she did not see him.

He had a picture of her in a summer frock which was the green of the Spring leaves, holding a tiny baby wrapped in a shawl against her breast.

She was looking down at it.

There was an expression in her eyes which made him think she might have been the Mother of God holding the infant Jesus.

The world seemed to stand still.

The Earl knew that this was what he wanted, this was what he had sought and had at last found.

One day he knew Ansella would hold his son in her arms and look as beautiful as she did at that moment.

Then Mrs. Shepherd, who was sitting beside an eldly woman, turned her head and saw the Earl.

"It's His Lordship!" she exclaimed, and began to rise to her feet.

Ansella also looked up.

She smiled and said to the Earl:

"May I present to Your Lordship the first baby born on your Estate since you returned from India. His Mother is very eager that you should be his Godfather."

"Of course," the Earl replied, "but only if you are his Godmother."

Ansella gave a little laugh.

"I will be delighted."

She moved through the door which the Earl knew led to a bedroom at the back.

147

He shook hands with the woman beside Mrs. Shep
herd, who he gathered was the Grandmother of th
newly born baby.

"It's glad us are that ye're back, M'Lord," she said a
she curtsied. "Us're all thanking God that ye wer
spared to be wit'us again."

She spoke very emotionally, and the Earl said quickl

"You must be delighted with your grandson. Is h
your first?"

"No, Oi've four already," the woman answered. "A
Oi'm hoping 'tis true that Yer Lordship be giving us
School."

"They will start building it immediately," the Ea
said.

He spoke with a positiveness which surprised himse

Then he was aware that if, as seemed very likely, Lo
Frazer died or did not recover from his stroke, Ansel
would have his huge fortune to administer.

She would certainly want him to provide a School f
the children in this village, also, doubtless, in the oth
villages as well.

He had been thinking as he rode away from Watte
Hall that he would have the administration of the lar
to see to.

Now he knew there would be enough money to pr
vide the two Estates with everything that was necessa
for the people who lived on them.

At the back of his mind was the uncomfortable feeli
that he was taking advantage of Lord Frazer's illness

At the same time, he told himself almost defiantly th
the people who served him must come first.

What could be more important than that their childr
were well fed and well educated?

Ansella came out of the bedroom smiling.

"The baby's Mother thanks you from her heart," s
said, "and we will arrange the Christening in two
three weeks time."

They said goodbye to the Grandmother.

When they went out, the Earl stopped to speak to some of the men who were working on various cottages.

They were delighted with his praise and as he went towards *Star* Ansella said:

"Do you think perhaps when they have finished we might give them a party?"

"Of course we will," the Earl agreed, "and I feel it might also celebrate our Marriage."

He was aware that Ansella looked at him questioningly.

Then there was a faint blush on her cheeks as she looked away.

She did not say anything.

As he rode back to the Castle he wondered what she was thinking.

'I have to make her love me,' he told himself.

He knew he was afraid of frightening her.

If she was frightened, she might turn away from him.

Yet he felt in his heart that the Viceroy was telling him to be patient and, if he was, the right moment would come.

"I only hope it will be soon," the Earl murmured beneath his breath.

He arrived back at the Castle at the same time as Ansella with Mrs. Shepherd in the carriage.

As he walked into the house behind his wife he longed to take her into his arms.

"It is time for you to have your bath," Ansella said as they reached the bottom of the stairs. "It was very kind of you to say you would be a Godfather to that baby. It was so small and sweet, and I wished I could keep it for myself."

With difficulty the Earl prevented himself from saying he would give her one of her own.

Instead, as they walked up the stairs he said:

"Your idea of a party is a very good one, and of course we must have fireworks."

"The children will love that," Ansella said, "and so will I."

"Then you will have the biggest and best fireworks obtainable," the Earl said.

"That will be another dream come true," she answered. "I used to beg Papa that I might have fireworks at Christmas, but he always refused. I think just because I wanted them."

The Earl had no wish to discuss Lord Frazer at that moment.

He therefore changed the subject before he went into his bedroom and Ansella into hers.

Because she was feeling happy, she chose a very pretty gown to wear which the Earl had not seen before.

In fact, when she came downstairs he could not think at first of any words to describe her.

Because he was silent, she said:

"I put this gown on to please you. Is anything wrong?"

"Everything is entirely right," the Earl said, "and you look very lovely and very ethereal."

"What does that mean?" she asked.

"It means that you might disappear into a cloud, or perhaps the lake, and then I would lose you."

She gave a little laugh.

"You will not do that. I am so happy here with you. It is very exciting doing things I have never been allowed to do before, like visiting that nice woman in the cottage and to be the first person to see her baby after it was born."

The Earl felt that no other woman he knew would have been so thrilled with someone else's child.

He could only imagine that Ansella would feel the same when he gave her a son of her own.

As they went into dinner he was praying again in his heart that it would not be long.

At the same time, the expression in Ansella's eyes as she talked to him was not yet what he wanted to see.

They talked about the things they were going to do, such as the School he was going to build.

But the conversation kept returning to the baby.

"It cannot just have your name," Ansella said. "We must think of another so that he has two, to make him seem important."

The Earl then suggested ridiculous names, some of them Indian, which made her laugh.

Then dinner was finished and they went into the Drawing-Room.

The room now looked very different from when he had first returned.

Cosnat, to please Ansella, had produced every flower he could and they were in vases.

The honeysuckle and the first roses that had come into bloom scented the air.

The Earl knew that, incredible though it seemed, he had found someone to take his Mother's place.

Ansella would fill it just as efficiently, charmingly, and lovingly as she had.

'But she has to love me,' his heart told him.

That way still seemed to be closed, and he was too frightened to jump it.

"Never rush your fences," the Viceroy had said to him once.

It was something he had always remembered.

He was telling Ansella that the next day he would arrange for the Family Portraits to be brought back.

They had been stored in Oxford while the Gallery was being repaired.

The door opened and Marlow came in.

He was carrying his usual silver salver on which there was a letter.

"This has arrived from the village, M'Lord," he said, holding it out to the Earl. "The Postman intended to bring it up with the other letters tomorrow morning, but he thinks as it's from America, Your Lordship should have it at once."

"That is very kind of him," the Earl said. "Tell him I appreciate the thought, and of course give him a drink before hc leaves."

Marlow smiled.

"I thinks that's what Your Lordship would order and I've already given 'im a glass of beer."

"Quite right," the Earl approved.

He was aware that a big barrel of beer had been brought to the Castle after he had told Mrs. Marlow to order anything she required.

He had made no comment when Marlow had served him at dinner with excellent white wine.

It was the same wine which his Father had always bought from his Wine-Merchant in Oxford.

As the Butler left the room, the Earl said to Ansella:

"Marlow thinks of everything."

"He thinks of you, as they all do," Ansella said, "and it is very touching."

She did not add, the Earl was thinking, that no one at Watton Hall would have dared to order anything without her Father's permission, however necessary they thought it was.

The Earl knew that in the eyes of Marlow and his wife he was still a small boy.

He had to be looked after, and they must think for him rather than let him think for himself.

It was indeed touching, and he was delighted that Ansella had realised it.

Then he looked at the letter which he held in his hand and saw it was, as Marlow said, from America.

He could not believe that his Uncle was writing to him.

Yet he could not think of anyone else he knew in America.

He felt certain that if it was from his Uncle, it contained bad news, and he was reluctant to open it.

He had enjoyed his dinner with Ansella and she was looking so happy and so lovely in her pretty gown that he did not want to spoil it.

He could not imagine what could have gone wrong.

But if his Uncle Basil was prepared to communicate with him, he must be wanting something.

Could it be possible that he had gone through all the money he had taken with him so quickly?

Had he already managed to be as crooked in America as he had been in England?

Was he in prison and needed his help, or had he perhaps been frightened by thieves and Blackmailers?

It all raced through the Earl's head until Ansella said with a little cry:

"What is the matter, you are looking worried! What has upset you?"

"I am not upset," the Earl said, "only apprehensive."

"Because you have had a letter from America? Oh, Michael, surely you do not think that horrible, wicked Uncle of yours is trying to get more than he has already."

"I do not know what it is," the Earl answered. "I know only that if we had a fire burning, I would throw the letter into it."

"No, that would be a mistake," Ansella said quickly as if she really meant it.

"Why?" the Earl asked out of curiosity.

"Because for the rest of your life you would always wonder what had been in the letter, and if perhaps instead of being bad news it was good news."

"I think that is most unlikely," the Earl said. "But of course, you are right. I must be brave, as you were brave yesterday, and open it."

"I was brave," Ansella said, "because I wanted to save you."

"Which you did very effectively," the Earl said. "Do you realise we might have been shut up there all night waiting this morning, cold and hungry, for someone to find the horses and then us."

"It is no use thinking about it," Ansella said, "because it did not happen. I shall never be sorry again that I am so thin, and so able to wriggle through that window."

She gave a little laugh before she said:

"When Papa kept telling me how skinny I was, I prayed I would get fat. Even when I ate lots of potatoes and sugar I still did not have to let out my waistband."

The Earl laughed.

"Most women would be thrilled to look like you. In fact, so many women I have known have pushed aside chocolates and iced cakes and pecked at their food when they longed to gobble it up because they were frightened of being fat."

"That is one worry I do not have," Ansella said, "and because you ride and take so much exercise, I cannot imagine you weighing down your horse or puffing when you walk up the stairs to bed."

The Earl thought that was just the sort of amusing thing she would say, and he laughed before he replied:

"Very well, I accept that we are both thin and brave, so I will open this letter. If it is bad news, we must try not to go to bed in tears."

"I hate your Uncle!" Ansella declared. "Why should he . . . upset us now when we are . . . so happy."

"Are you happy?" the Earl asked.

"Very . . . very . . . happy," she answered. "I think your Castle is enchanted, and everyone who comes into it feels they have been touched by a magic wand so that they want to laugh and dance and sing with joy."

With difficulty the Earl prevented himself from putting out his arms.

He had never heard her speak like this before.

It thrilled him in a way that was quite indescribable.

"That is the nicest compliment the Castle has ever been paid," he said, "and if it could bow, it would undoubtedly do so."

"Then let us believe," Ansella said, "that whatever is in the letter, the Castle magic will prevent it from upsetting us."

She rose as she spoke and went to the desk and brought back a letter-opener.

It was not the gold one which the Earl's Father had used.

Uncle Basil had sold or taken that away with him.

It was quite an ordinary opener provided by Marlow.

The Earl slit the top of the envelope and drew out what seemed a very long letter.

A glance at the top of it told him it was from a firm of Solicitors.

Once again he was apprehensive that his Uncle was in trouble.

He told himself after the way Basil Burne had behaved he was under no obligation to do anything for him, no matter how urgent it might seem!

Then he began to read the letter.

He was aware as he did so that Ansella was watching him.

He thought she expected him to read it aloud or to make some comment.

Instead, after he had read a few lines he read as quickly as he could what came next.

He turned over the first page and then the second.

It was only when he came to the end that he put down the letter and said:

"I just do not believe it."

"What has happened?" Ansella asked.

Now there was a note of anxiety in her voice.

"I think I must be dreaming," the Earl replied. "Things do not happen like this in real life."

"What has he done? You must . . . tell me!"

The Earl picked up the letter again.

"This is from some Solicitors in Dallas," he said slowly, "who have written to inform me that Mr. Basil Burne has had an accident when he was riding a horse in a Rodeo."

"An accident?" Ansella questioned.

"According to this letter, he insisted on riding although advised not to do so, and the horse, which was a very spirited one, threw him and he broke his spine."

"So he is dead," Ansella said in a whisper.

"He is dead," the Earl confirmed.

For a moment Ansella did not speak, and he went on:

"The Solicitors were intelligent enough to find out that I am head of the family and they now inform me that as my Uncle left no Will I am expected to claim what money he has left and the Estate he had recently bought in that part of America."

"In Dallas?" Ansella questioned.

"In Dallas," the Earl confirmed, "and before he died he had just found oil on it."

Ansella stared at him.

"That was the reason he had a Rodeo and I imagine had drunk a great deal to celebrate his discovery."

"But . . . he is . . . dead," Ansella said as if she could hardly believe it.

"He is dead," the Earl replied, "and now everything he stole from me will be returned as soon as I apply for it, and the Solicitors are only too eager to do that on my instructions."

"So you . . . will get . . . back your . . . money?"

Ansella spoke in a low voice, and the Earl said:

"What I find hard to believe, and I am sure you will feel the same, is that I do not only get back everything my Uncle stole from me, which is a very considerable sum, but the fact he had found oil has made his Estate extremely valuable."

He looked at the last page of the letter and said in a voice which hardly sounded like his own:

"In fact, his Solicitors tell me that his assets at a quick valuation are approximately two million pounds."

He found it difficult to say the words himself.

In fact, he looked again at the last page of the letter in case he had made a mistake.

"Yes, that is right," he said. "Two million pounds!"

He spoke slowly.

Then, as he looked up from the letter, he heard Ansella give a little cry.

To his astonishment, she went across the room and out through the door.

"Ansella!" he exclaimed. "Where are you going?"

She did not answer, and he got to his feet.

He was aware as he did so that *Rufus*, who had been curled up asleep by the sofa, had followed Ansella.

Puzzled, the Earl walked to the door.

"Ansella," he called again.

He went out into the passage.

He saw with surprise that she was not in the hall or walking up the stairs towards her bedroom.

He turned to look the other way and just saw *Rufus* disappearing at the far end of the long corridor.

For a moment he was puzzled.

Then a sudden idea struck him.

He started to walk, at first quickly, down the corridor, then he ran.

He felt as if someone were telling him that Ansella was in danger.

He ran as quickly as he could until he reached, as he expected to do, the door to the Tower.

It was open.

He hurried up the spiral stairs.

When he reached the top, the door, like the one below, was open.

Ansella was on the other side of the Tower.

She was looking over the balustrade down into the moat.

With the swiftness of an athlete, the Earl reached her and put his arms around her.

"What are you doing? Why did you come here?" he asked.

She put out her hands to push him away from her.

"You are ... not to ... stop me," she said. "I have ... got to ... die ... I would ... rather ... die than ... live without ... you."

"My Darling, what are you talking about?" the Earl asked.

"Now that ... you have ... got your money ... you will ... not want ... me ... anymore," she said in a sobbing little voice. "And perhaps ... you will ... send me back ... to Papa."

The Earl tightened his arms around her.

"How could you think of anything so crazy and absurd?" he asked. "How could you want to leave me in such a wicked way?"

"I ... love you ... I love ... you," Ansella said wildly, "and I would ... rather ... die than ... go on living ... without you."

The Earl bent his head and found her lips.

He kissed her not gently, but fiercely, as he thought she might have drowned herself as she intended to do.

For a moment she was still.

Then he felt her lips respond, and her whole body seemed to melt into his.

He kissed her and went on kissing her until they were both breathless.

Then at length he raised his head.

"How could you leave me?" he asked.

"It ... is ... because I ... love ... you," Ansella answered a little incoherently.

"As I love you," he answered.

"You ... love ... me?"

It was a question which sounded almost like the song of a bird.

"I have loved you for a long time, my Precious," the Earl said, "but I have been desperately afraid of frightening you. So I have been waiting. Waiting, I may say, very impatiently, until you loved me."

"I do ... love ... you ... I love ... you with all ... my heart and ... my soul," Ansella said. "I have never known what it ... is to be ... happy ... before."

"We shall be very happy together for the rest of our lives," the Earl said. "But, my Darling, you must trust me. How could you think for a moment I would let you go back to your Father."

"You did ... not want ... to marry ... me," Ansella said in a very small voice. "You ... wanted only the ... money Papa gave you ... for me."

"That was before I knew you," the Earl answered. "I was thinking today I was the luckiest man in the whole world because I had found what all men seek."

"You ... mean ... love?" Ansella asked.

"I mean the perfect woman," he said, "and that, my Precious, is you. To me you are completely and absolutely perfect and just as you love me with your heart, I love you with mine."

"Oh ... Michael."

Tears were running down Ansella's cheeks, and he knew they were tears of joy.

The Earl realised now how much she had suffered thinking he had wanted her only for her money.

When he had told her the contents of the letter from America, it was for her the voice of doom, taking her back to the misery and cruelty of her Father.

"Oh, my Precious, Adorable, Darling little wife," the Earl said, "now that I know you love me, I have so much to tell you and so much to teach you, and it is up here, of all places, on the Tower that we are starting our real married life together."

He kissed her again.

Then he gently drew her across the top of the Tower.

They went down the steps.

When they were half-way down, the Earl stopped and opened a door which led onto the first floor.

It was a door which was very seldom used.

Everyone visiting the Tower had always started at the bottom so as to see the Guard Room.

Now he drew Ansella out on to the corridor on which their bedrooms were situated.

*Rufus*, who had followed them, went ahead as if to show them the way.

It passed through the Earl's mind that if he had not saved her from what she had intended to do, all he would have been left with would have been *Rufus*.

He took Ansella into her bedroom, and then he said:

"Tomorrow, my Precious, I am going to move you into my Mother's room which, as you know, is on the other side of mine. I know now that you are exactly the person she would have chosen to be my wife, and that you will take her place here at the Castle and make it a house of love for everyone who comes to it."

"Oh, Michael, can . . . I do . . . that?" Ansella asked.

"I know you can," he answered, "and now, my Darling, I want you to get into bed."

"I do . . . not want . . . you to . . . leave me," she said, holding on to the revers of his coat.

He smiled.

"Do you really think I am going to leave you?" he asked. "I have wanted you almost unbearably for these last nights, and it was with the greatest difficulty that I did not come into your room and tell you how much I loved you."

"Oh ... why did ... you not ... do that? I was ... loving you and thought miserably ... you did not ... really want ... me but my—"

The Earl put his fingers over her mouth.

"You are never going to finish that sentence," he said. "We are never going to forget all the unhappiness we have been through and remember only that you saved me yesterday and I have saved you today because we love each other."

She hid her face against his neck and he kissed her hair.

"Get into bed, my Precious," he said. "I cannot wait any longer to hold you really close to me."

She looked up at him.

There was a radiance in her face which he had not seen before.

Then he went into his own room and hurriedly undressed.

He left the communicating-door open just in case she changed her mind and ran back to the Tower.

He could not believe she would do so.

Yet he was so afraid he might lose this wonderful magical moment he had just found and was taking no chances.

He went back into Ansella's room a very short time later.

He found the candles were all extinguished except for those by the bed.

Ansella had also drawn back the curtains so that he could see the stars which now filled the sky.

There was a half moon throwing its light over the garden.

Ansella watched the Earl coming towards her.

He thought with her fair hair falling over her shoulders she looked incredibly lovely, even more like the

Greek Goddess he had thought her to be.

He stood for a moment by the bed, looking down at her, and then he said:

"You are so lovely, so beautiful, my Darling, I cannot believe you are real."

"I am . . . real," Ansella said, "and . . . I love . . . you."

"As I love you," the Earl answered, "and that is why I am so afraid of frightening you."

"I am . . . not frightened . . . anymore," Ansella said. "How could I be . . . frightened of . . . you?"

The Earl took off his robe and, blowing out the candles, he got into bed.

He pulled her into his arms and said:

"This is what I have been longing for and was so afraid that you would not love me enough to let me touch you."

"I wanted . . . you to . . . kiss me," Ansella whispered, "but thought . . . perhaps you . . . loved someone . . . else."

"This is the truth," the Earl said. "I have never loved anyone as I love you and I never will."

He kissed her.

He felt her quiver with the rapture and the wonder of it.

He knew then that their love would carry them into a Paradise that was entirely their own.

They had found the love which came from God and was part of God.

The Earl knew he would always be eternally grateful for it.

"I love . . . you," he heard Ansella say. "You are so . . . brave . . . so kind and so . . . very . . . wonderful."

"And I love you, my beautiful, adorable, innocent little wife," the Earl said.

Then, as he kissed her again, there was no need for words.

They had found love, and love filled their whole world and the world beyond it.

162

## ABOUT THE AUTHOR

**Barbara Cartland,** the world's most famous romantic novelist, who is also an historian, playwright, lecturer, political speaker and television personality, has now written 613 books and sold over six hundred and twenty million copies all over the world.

She has also had many historical works published and has written four autobiographies as well as the biographies of her mother and that of her brother, Ronald Cartland, who was the first Member of Parliament to be killed in the last war. This book has a preface by Sir Winston Churchill and has been republished with an introduction by Sir Arthur Bryant.

*Love at the Helm*, a novel written with the help and inspiration of the late Earl Mountbatten of

Burma, Great Uncle of His Royal Highness, The Prince of Wales, is being sold for the Mountbatten Memorial Trust.

She has broken the world record for the last twenty-one years by writing an average of twenty-three books a year. In the *Guinness Book of World Records* she is listed as the world's top-selling author.

Miss Cartland in 1987 sang an Album of Love Songs with the Royal Philharmonic Orchestra.

In private life Barbara Cartland, who is a Dame of the Order of St. John of Jerusalem and Chairman of the St. John Council in Hertfordshire, has fought for better conditions and salaries for Midwives and Nurses.

She championed the cause for the Elderly in 1956, invoking a Government Enquiry into the "Housing Condition of Old People."

In 1962 she had the Law of England changed so that Local Authorities had to provide camps for their own Gypsies. This has meant that since then thousands and thousands of Gypsy children have been able to go to School, which they had never been able to do in the past, as their caravans were moved every twenty-four hours by the Police.

There are now fifteen camps in Hertfordshire and Barbara Cartland has her own Romany Gypsy Camp called "Barbaraville" by the Gypsies.

Her designs "Decorating with Love" are being sold all over the U.S.A. and the National Home Fashions League made her, in 1981, "Woman of Achievement."

She is unique in that she was one and two in the Dalton list of Best Sellers, and one week had four books in the top twenty.

Barbara Cartland's book *Getting Older, Growing Younger* has been published in Great Britain and the U.S.A. and her fifth cookery book, *The Romance of Food*, is now being used by the House of Commons.

In 1984 she received at Kennedy Airport America's Bishop Wright Air Industry Award for her contribution to the development of aviation. In 1931 she and two R.A.F. Officers thought of, and carried, the first aeroplane-towed glider airmail.

During the War she was Chief Lady Welfare Officer in Bedfordshire, looking after 20,000 Servicemen and -women. She thought of having a pool of Wedding Dresses at the War Office so a Service Bride could hire a gown for the day.

She bought 1,000 gowns without coupons for the A.T.S., the W.A.A.F.s and the W.R.E.N.S. In 1945 Barbara Cartland received the Certificate of Merit from Eastern Command.

In 1964 Barbara Cartland founded the National Association for Health of which she is the President, as a front for all the Health Stores and for any product made as alternative medicine.

This is now a £65 million turnover a year, with one-third going in export.

In January 1968 she received *La Médeille de Vermeil de la Ville de Paris*. This is the highest award to be given in France by the City of Paris.

She has sold 30 million books in France.

In March 1988 Barbara Cartland was asked by the Indian Government to open their Health Resort outside Delhi. This is almost the largest Health Resort in the world.

Barbara Cartland was received with great enthusiasm by her fans, who feted her at a reception in the City, and she received the gift of an embossed plate from the Government.

Barbara Cartland was made a Dame of the Order of the British Empire in the 1991 New Year's Honours List by Her Majesty, The Queen, for her contribution to Literature and also for her years of work for the community.

Dame Barbara has now written 613 books, the greatest number by a British author, passing the 564 books written by John Creasey.

## AWARDS

1945    Received Certificate of Merit, Eastern Command, for being Welfare Officer to 5,000 troops in Bedfordshire.

1953    Made a Commander of the Order of St. John of Jerusalem. Invested by H.R.H. The Duke of Gloucester at Buckingham Palace.

1972    Invested as Dame of Grace of the Order of St. John in London by The Lord Prior, Lord Cacia.

1981    Received "Achiever of the Year" from the National Home Furnishing Association in Colorado Springs, U.S.A., for her designs for wallpaper and fabrics.

1984    Received Bishop Wright Air Industry Award at Kennedy Airport, for inventing the aeroplane-towed Glider.

1988    Received from Monsieur Chirac, The Prime Minister, The Gold Medal of the City of Paris, at the Hotel de la Ville, Paris, for selling 25 million books and giving a lot of employment.

1991    Invested as Dame of the Order of The British Empire, by H.M. The Queen at Buckingham Palace for her contribution to Literature.